P9-BYZ-869

"You look wonderful in that peach satin," Cas murmured. "You glow."

When she turned and smiled, her gaze sensual and inviting, he froze. That look! Margo used to have that look. Don't think of her, he warned himself.

"Headache?" she asked huskily.

"No," he said. "I was just wondering how you'd react if I carried you up the stairs and made mad, passionate love to you right now." As soon as he'd said it, he wished he could call it back. It was too soon. . . .

"Why don't you try and see?" she asked. The idea was so delicious she was ready to drag him bodily there herself.

"Try what?" he asked, unbelieving.

"Have you forgotten so soon?" She smiled. "Well, why don't we have a drink first? You could loosen your tie . . . and other things," she teased.

He couldn't breathe, couldn't move. She mustn't have believed he was serious. Her answer had been provocative, and flirtatious, but innocent too. He would have to be careful with her, he decided. "Champagne?"

"Yes, please." She sipped from the glass he handed her. "It's good." She paused. "But there are tastier things."

Moving close to her, he took the glass from her hand. "True. I'd like to taste you." Her lazy smile set him on fire.

"Shall I pour champagne on myself, or would you like me plain?" she asked.

"Either way," he murmured, then touched her lips with his. . . .

WHAT ARE *LOVESWEPT* ROMANCES?

They are stories of true romance and touching emotion. We believe those two very important ingredients are constants in our highly sensual and very believable stories in the *LOVESWEPT* line. Our goal is to give you, the reader, stories of consistently high quality that may sometimes make you laugh, sometimes make you cry, but are always fresh and creative and contain many delightful surprises within their pages.

Most romance fans read an enormous number of books. Those they truly love, they keep. Others may be traded with friends and soon forgotten. We hope that each *LOVESWEPT* romance will be a treasure—a "keeper." We will always try to publish

LOVE STORIES YOU'LL NEVER FORGET
BY AUTHORS YOU'LL ALWAYS REMEMBER

The Editors

LOVESWEPT® • 455

Helen Mittermeyer
The Mask

BANTAM BOOKS
NEW YORK • TORONTO • LONDON • SYDNEY • AUCKLAND

THE MASK

A Bantam Book / February 1991

LOVESWEPT® and the wave device are registered
trademarks of Bantam Books, a division of
Bantam Doubleday Dell Publishing Group, Inc.
Registered in U.S. Patent
and Trademark Office and elsewhere.

All rights reserved.
Copyright © 1991 by Helen Mittermeyer.
Cover art copyright © 1991 by Hal Frenck.
No part of this book may be reproduced or transmitted
in any form or by any means, electronic or mechanical,
including photocopying, recording, or by any information
storage and retrieval system, without permission in
writing from the publisher.
For information address: Bantam Books.

If you would be interested in receiving protective vinyl
covers for your Loveswept books, please write to this
address for information:

Loveswept
Bantam Books
P. O. Box 985
Hicksville, NY 11802

ISBN 0-553-44100-0

Published simultaneously in the United States and Canada

Bantam Books are published by Bantam Books, a division
of Bantam Doubleday Dell Publishing Group, Inc. Its trademark, consisting of the words "Bantam Books" and the
portrayal of a rooster, is Registered in U.S. Patent and
Trademark Office and in other countries. Marca Regis-
trada. Bantam Books, 666 Fifth Avenue, New York, New
York 10103.

PRINTED IN THE UNITED STATES OF AMERICA

OPM   0 9 8 7 6 5 4 3 2 1

To men and women who hide themselves, for whatever reason. For even when they do, they're real.

And to my children, Paul, Ann, Daniel, Cristy, daughter-in-law Markey, and granddaughter, Kendra.

Prologue

1978

"I tell you she's too young to see fortune-tellers and such things. She's terribly upset, Ione."

"Really, Ivor, you're ridiculous about the girl. She's fifteen and mature enough to understand that it's nonsense."

"A charlatan tells her she'll die young and be stripped of all unnecessary life, then be reborn, and you say she can handle that?"

"You're roaring like a bull, Ivor, and I resent it. After all, I'm your wife."

"And Margo became my child at the death of her parents. I won't allow anything to hurt her. Remember that, Ione."

"You can't orchestrate her entire life. Remember that, Ivor."

One

November 1988

The sun glinted on the water, making it look like a rippling stream of pure gold. The brightness hurt the eyes. Florida gulls swooped and cried in their everlasting hunt for food. The trees on shore bent and swayed in rhythmic answer to the breeze. All creatures great and small exulted in the joy of living on a perfect morning.

Doom and gloom, however, assailed Lancaster McCross Griffith. As though a devil walked over his grave, Cas shuddered, goose-bumps rising on his skin. In a flash he saw his life turn a corner, explode with light. Everything changed. New direction. Rubbing his hand across his eyes, he shook his head. Imagination, he told himself. His mind playing tricks. Or a hangover. Late nights, cards, and Jack Daniel's could do that.

Cas yawned and squinted at the beautiful,

serene environment. Damn! he thought. It was an irritating nirvana, mindless and boring. Nettles of restlessness bored into him. He was tired, but couldn't sleep, feeling too nervous, on the brink of something. And he didn't want to be there. He leaned against a dock stanchion, wincing at the sudden stabbing behind his eyes. Maybe he should have slept for a couple of hours, instead of leaving the card table, going to his room to change his clothes, and then signing out a boat. The card game hadn't broken-up until past dawn. He'd kept a relatively clear head, as he always did when gambling, but he'd drunk enough Jack Daniel's to wish he'd stuck to Saratoga water all night, instead of just at the end.

He closed his eyes behind his sunglasses and willed his head to clear. Why the hell was he in Florida instead of Aspen, Colorado, which was where he wanted to be? Damn the sunshine, the cool breeze, the heat on his back. He wanted snow, schussing, blue spruces reaching to the sky, mountains pushing past them into the puffs of cloud, and powder deeper than a man was tall. Sighing, he arched away from the stanchion.

His headache started at his ankles and had a blues beat by the time it reached his neck. As he rubbed it, he wished he'd given his father a stronger argument against coming south. Joining his parents and their friends at the posh Grand Palm Inn had not been a high priority. He'd wanted a week of exercise with women and skiing, with a heavy emphasis on both. Instead, he was in the throes of a familial two-step engineered by his father. Dammit, he loved the man, but at times . . . Cas ground his teeth together and shaded his eyes.

The rising sun was going to be hot, but right now the air was balmy enough. He'd figured that instead of sacking out and waking up with a big head, he'd be smart and let a sailor's breeze take it all away. Now he doubted the wisdom of his decision.

Ambling down the long dock, he stopped at the sailboats. He acknowledged the sultry smile of the blond attendant who pointed out his boat to him. She was very attractive, but at the moment, sailing the Hobie Cat was more important to him. The wind in his face could alleviate the drum concerto in his head and might even settle his churning stomach. Rigging the sail quickly, he climbed down onto the twin-hulled boat, grabbed the tiller, and pushed away from the dock. The light but steady breeze belled out the sail, but not enough to challenge his skill as the craft heeled over a degree to starboard. Stretching out his long body, he grasped the tiller loosely and headed out the marina canal to the Seven Seas Lagoon.

As he sailed, he looked up, blinking at the pristine blue sky. The surroundings were an easy distraction, he admitted. Not snow-covered mountains, but pleasant. Lazily he steered out of the docking channel into the lagoon. His momentary black mood would soon dissipate.

Since it was early and most guests wouldn't be up and out until much later in the morning, there weren't many boats on the water. A few of the small single-passenger motorboats common to the man-made waterway were his only companions.

Out in the middle of the lagoon the breeze stiffened, and the cat lifted and responded, heeling over again. Cas sighed happily, his eyes almost closing. Ah! Soon his headache would vanish. The hiss and rippling sounds the craft made cutting through the water soothed his twanging nerves. The sounds wouldn't have even been audible if he hadn't been a distance from other boats. Well-being seeped into his pores. Coming out for a sail had been the right thing to do after all.

He refused to allow the sound of an approaching motor interrupt his reverie. The boat would pass him by, then it would be quiet again. When the sound became a low roar, he glanced over his shoulder, then did a double take.

"Hey! What the hell . . . ?" One of the damned put-puts was heading right at him.

"Give way, dammit," Cas called out angrily, even as he yanked at the sheets to bring the cat about, so that it would take a perpendicular tack away from the motorboat.

The boat veered the same way. The person driving the boat was standing up, looking over the windscreen, waving and mouthing something. What the hell was the matter with him? Didn't the guy understand that unmotorized crafts had the right of way?

Cas tried to change his course again, knowing he wouldn't have time. The damn thing was coming too fast. And right at him! He leaned out as far as he could to yank the bow back, hoping the fool would steer around him. Scrambling, he got to the port side of the cat—then the motorboat hit, dead center on the starboard, catching it under the pontoon. The cat shuddered, sluiced, and angled upward.

Cas cursed, struggling to stay aboard. One of the sheets tangled on him, the boom swung, the boat careened again. Then, arms and legs flailing, he smacked the water face first, went under, and swallowed quarts. Surfacing, coughing, he shouted angrily and got another mouthful. Before he could come up again, someone grabbed a fistful of his hair.

"Don't worry, sir. I have you," a female voice said in his ear, the hand pulling his hair harder.

"Dammit, let go of my hair, I'm not drowning." Cas grabbed his head when she released him. Where the hell did she get off calling him sir? How old was she?

"Then what are you doing?" she asked, "Trying out for *La Traviata?* You were screeching like a stuck pig, for heaven's sake."

Her amused observation had him grinding his teeth. He let go of the cat line and grabbed the side of the motorboat. "Listen, you—" Even through his ire he saw she was lovely, beautifully rounded with skin smooth as cream. Wet black hair slapped across the darkest blue eyes he'd ever seen. A sensuous cherub.

"Your sailboat is going bye-bye," she said.

"What?" Cas spun around and stroked after the cat, which was bobbing away from him. His strong crawl ate up the distance, but suddenly the sailboat started moving faster. He redoubled his efforts, more than anything because he wanted to get back to that gorgeous angel.

"Don't worry," the woman called. "I'll get it!"

Margo still wasn't quite sure how to handle the motorboat, but she was getting better. Whoops, she thought. She'd have to make sure not to get too close to people. She might have scraped the crabby man's shoulder just then. Even though he was crabby, he had a handsome face and marvelous emerald eyes. He didn't seem as old as she'd thought at first, and he certainly was sexy.

"No . . . Aagh." Cas swallowed more water when the sexy brat with the navy-blue eyes and creamy skin just missed him as she chased after the cat. Instead of corralling the boat, she banged into it, time after time. "Wait! Will you hold it? I've got it." He grabbed one of the sheets, glaring at his would-be boat rescuer. "Thanks." She was a beautiful disaster. And his headache was gone.

"You're welcome." Therapy might help his irascibility, Margo thought.

Heaving himself across the twin-hulled craft, Cas turned, tiller in hand to gaze at his nemesis. "Do you always attack sailboats?" Damn, she was beautiful. There was a fragile, almost oriental look to her, though she was full-bodied and curvaceous. She was nothing like the skinny model types he usually dated. Those wonderful breasts pushing out of her bikini were perfection. The thought of kissing them made him gasp.

"I heard that," she said. "Were you hurt? Are you in pain? Did you bang yourself getting aboard? Maybe you should get some instruction in sailing, sir." Lord, he was a hunk, Margo thought. His shoulders were like bronze satin. What would it be like to rub her hands over that skin? That made her hot all over. Lord! The man was magical.

"I crewed in the America's Cup," he said tautly, then regretted saying anything when her smile widened. "And don't call me sir," he muttered through his teeth.

"Your father buy you in for a ride in the Cup?" she asked. Laughter bubbled out of her. He was cute when he was riled.

Her amusement turned Cas upside down, sent his libido and blood pressure rocketing. Her smile was angelic . . . and devilish. It took away his annoyance. "No."

His reluctant grin made her heart flip like a landed fish. Was she melting? Had she ever met such a man? "I'm not very good at this."

"I noticed." He curled the line around his wrist and touched the tiller, steering closer to her boat, grabbing her mooring line. "Can you swim?" At her nod, he inhaled and studied her. He liked the way her eyes lifted at the outer corners, as though she'd had an oriental ancestor. "Like to go for a sail? It might be safer."

Margo studied him in turn, leaning on the side of the boat. He had a small scar that curved upward on his left eyebrow. Very sexy, very piratical. Could she trust him? Why did she feel so safe? It was insanity. "Might be a mistake to take up with strangers in a sailboat." Was that a dimple at the corner of his mouth? His hair was like old gold and glinted blond and red. "What would I do with my boat?"

He shrugged. "I'll follow you back to the dock and we can leave it at the Grand Palm Inn."

"How do you know I'm staying there?" Funny the way her heart was bumping against her ribs. And to think she'd fought Uncle Ivor about coming to Florida. She'd had the feeling he was trying one more time to get her together with the son of one of his friends.

"I don't know you're staying there," Cas answered. "But I am, and they won't mind." Where was she staying? he wondered. He needed to know that.

"All right. I guess I'd better know your name. I can't keep calling you Stranger in Sailboat."

"I'm Cas." Watching as she tried to turn her boat and hit his sailboat again, he laughed.

"I'm Margo. What's so funny?"

"Waiting for you to dock that thing might take time. We could end up sailing at night."

"That's what you think." Whipping the wheel around, Margo almost tipped herself out. Then, the boat rocking wildly, she steered a halfway straight course toward the dock at the Grand Palm Inn. She glanced over her shoulder. Damn him. He was still laughing. She wasn't sorry he'd been dunked in the lagoon.

Still, she couldn't contain a grin. She hadn't even known she was cold until Cas warmed her. She'd not been aware of a void in her life until he smiled. This was no cloying barnacle who jumped to do his father's bidding like others she'd known. This was a man . . . from the sea. And he didn't know her, or anything about her. Intriguing.

In a shorter time than she'd hoped, even with a great deal of twisting and turning, she was heading down the docking canal to the Grand Palm Inn. When she reached the space allotted to her, she held her breath, aimed herself toward it, steering a bit frantically, then entered and turned off the motor. The thump against the mooring almost gave her a whiplash. Somehow, some way, she vowed she'd get the hang of handling a boat before she went back to New York. Ignoring the bemused stare of the attendant, she stepped onto the wharf and turned to look for Cas. He was right behind her. Lord, he was a gorgeous sight, she thought, sprawled across the twin-hulled boat that way. She could almost smell his electric power. Heady stuff! The female attendants were grinning from ear to ear, rushing toward the end of the wharf nearest him. Damn them. They'd made little attempt to help her. Margo strolled after them.

"So you do belong here," Cas murmured, his words carrying around the girls, reverberating over the water. She was gorgeous, her legs long and sexy, her body full, rich looking, sensuous. He couldn't stop staring at her.

"Yes." His lean, tough face didn't reveal his thoughts, Margo noted. He had a wild sophistication, as though civilization were just a thin patina that he could shed at will. She felt as if she were looking back, back into the past. Cas was Eric the Red's descendant who'd appeared on a Hobie Cat. He was a Yankee Viking. And that broad chest sprinkled with auburn-gold hair was pure Viking. Only the beard was missing.

"Come aboard," he invited. Damn, he thought, he couldn't recall ever being this sexually intrigued this fast. Had he ever wanted any woman so badly, so soon? The hell with analyzing. She was here, with him. That was enough for now. He would take it slow with her. There was an ingenuousness behind her captivating smile. It dictated that she needed cosseting not rushing.

At first Margo felt self-conscious lying next to him on the small canvas deck suspended between the two pontoons. They didn't touch, but there was enough heat and lightning between them to fire a booster rocket at Canaveral. The air was charged with their closeness.

Lord, she thought, she should've worn a one-piece suit. It would be more slimming, and she wasn't a slim person. Her hips were too wide, breasts too full. No matter what it took, she'd diet this year. What was he thinking? Thunder thighs, probably. Aaagh! Oh, to be thin. He wasn't thin. He was big, muscular, sleek. He was beautiful. What would it be like to lean against that muscular chest? Now, she was sweating. Be cool, she told herself. She pushed back the wet strands of her hair. Heavy and thick, it always took so long to dry. Damn, it was stringy. *Dry, dry,* she ordered it.

Cas followed the movement of her hand and arm, noting how her full breasts tautened, how her black hair settled on her white shoulders. Incredible. His body tensed in beginning arousal. In his Riviera briefs it'd be difficult to hide.

"We're staring at each other," he said ruefully. "I like what I see. I hope you do."

"Blunt, aren't you?" Margo hoped he couldn't discern the hard thumping of her heart. Too much of her skin was showing. She was definitely going to work out more. Oh, for a one-piece. She stared up into the rigging, trying to get herself back on balance. "Nice boat."

"Right." She wasn't married, he thought. No ring. But didn't some women not wear rings? "How old are you?"

"Huh? Why?" Her head snapped down and she stared at him.

"There's heat between us. I don't want to be involved with a teenager." Where did that come from? Damn! Talk about rushing! He ground his teeth. Rarely did he feel off the mark with a woman. Now he could sense the run of blood up his neck. Dammit, he was acting like a school kid. Whatever happened to the vow he'd made about going it alone? No responsibilities except to himself and his work. A life's commitment changing in minutes! Insanity.

"What?" Margo reared up, lost her balance, and slid off the boat into the lagoon. Thrashing, she rose to the surface, spluttering. She felt Cas's strong arm around her middle, lifting her up. "You . . . did . . . that . . . on purpose. To . . . pay . . . me back." She coughed, choked, swiped at her eyes, but remained in the water, liking his arm around her.

Cas let go of the lines. The sail luffed, the boat drifted. Lying on his stomach, leaning over the gunwales, he put his other hand at her waist. It was wonderful. He felt so good, he laughed out loud. "For what it's worth," he said, "I didn't say that to dump you in the water and pay you back. It came out of nowhere. But I'm not calling it back, either."

In fact, he wanted to see her for breakfast and lunch, today, tomorrow . . . His mouth was inches from hers. It seemed natural to kiss her, letting his mouth open on hers, his tongue questing. When she parted her lips and her tongue touched his, blood thundered through his veins, the power of it threatening to overwhelm him. It was like dying just to kiss her. Without releasing her mouth, he tightened his grip on her and heaved her upward, out of the water, turning at the same time. When he lowered her, she was on top of him. He released her mouth, watching her, keeping her atop him. "Very powerful, my Margo."

"I'm not yours," she said squeakily, her heart hammered so hard, she could barely swallow or take a breath. Weakly resting her head on his chest, she felt the thudding of his own heart. He wasn't as unaffected as he seemed. "This is crazy. I'm too heavy. Let me go."

"Umm. Never. You're just right." Cas held her, his eyes closed, feeling an alien contentment that defied description. *Happiness* was not a word he applied to himself. *Useful, ambitious, triumphant, confident* were all the buzz words. At that moment he was so supremely joyous, he shook with delight. Damn, he had to slow down. He could lose her. That, he couldn't deal with. He had to pull back, but his hands wouldn't follow the directions his brain gave them.

Margo wriggled closer, smiling when she heard him groan. It was only a moment in time, she thought. Maybe there'd be no more. She would savor what she had. Hell, she was twenty-five. She'd always craved more. Of what? Her career as a junior account executive in Uncle Ivor's brokerage firm was a job, no more. Business was interesting, but not absorbing. Deep down she'd always wanted to pursue her love of painting and sculpting that she'd dabbled in in high school and college, but she hadn't done it. She figured someday she would marry one of the members of Uncle Ivor's brain trust, or maybe even the son of a friend— and have a family. She didn't look for or expect rockets, fireworks, missiles of sexual delight when she did tie the knot. So, for now, why not indulge in a diversion?

"Baby, don't wriggle that way," Cas told her roughly. Damn, he wanted her. So fast, so much. She touched his shin with her toe, her nail gently abrading, and the blood bubbled through him. Then her leg massaged him and he gripped her to him. His mouth roved her cheek and neck. She licked the side of his face, the tactile sensation setting him on fire. The hoots and hollers of two passing boatmen pulled them apart.

Cas let her move back from him, but kept her atop him. Their gazes clung as though embracing just as their arms and legs did. It was sensuous, wonderful. Another boat passed. There was laughter.

Reluctantly, Cas let her roll off him, keeping her at his side. "Margo? Look at me." When she did, he smiled. "Something special happened on this cat."

"We both got dunked?" She smiled when he laughed.

"That too."

"Is this how we're going to sail?" She couldn't clear the hoarseness from her throat.

"Unless you object." He touched her forehead with his mouth. She smelled and tasted so very good.

"I don't object." It was madness. She didn't want him to let go.

They continued to sail, lying close to each other, shifting desultorily when the boat came about, oblivious of others or the passing time.

"Have dinner with me tonight," he whispered. He had to see her that evening . . . and tomorrow and the day after that.

"I'll try," Margo said, her mouth inches from his. He was too gorgeous to be real. His tongue touched the edge of her lips. She sighed and closed her eyes. "My uncle is having guests and he'll want me there." Uncle Ivor was going to be disappointed. Somehow she was going to dine with Cas.

"Get out of it. I have to reshuffle something myself. Say about eight?" He held his breath.

"All right." Uncle Ivor would throw a shoe. So? She wanted to have dinner with Cas and she would. Up the rebels.

The sun rose higher, its heat blistering. Margo pulled sun block from her net bag and offered it.

"You do me, I'll do you," Cas said huskily.

"All right."

Lathered in sun block they sailed, then cooled

off in the water, put on more sun block, watched each other, smiled all the time. It was heaven!

"No, Uncle Ivor, I won't stay for dinner," Margo said firmly. "I've made other plans. I will have a drink with your friends, but I'm meeting someone at eight, and I won't be late." She lifted her chin, staring at the man who'd raised and pampered her all her life.

"But Margo, my dear, you can't. The plans are made," Ivor Tyssen blustered, frustration and ire mottling his skin. "We'll talk more about this when we're having cocktails." He tugged at the folds of his bow tie.

"I think it's wonderful you've found some friends, dear," Ione Tyssen said, ignoring her husband's fulminating stare. "Will Bahira be coming with you?"

"Bahira?" Margo stared blankly at her aunt. Ione had been married to Ivor for over twenty years and ran her own lucrative interior-decorating business in Manhattan. Her face was unlined, and there was a serenity about her. She and her husband got along famously . . . unless they discussed Margo. The niece they both loved had been a bone of contention on many occasions.

Margo loved both her aunt and uncle. Now, she winced as the telltale signs of another family skirmish began to appear. "Bahira, did you say?" She hadn't given her best friend a thought all day. Cas had been on her mind.

"Really, Ione, I wish you wouldn't encourage her." Ivor was tall like his Swedish forebears. His hair, once blond, was now gray and thinning. But he carried himself straight and with all the confidence that money and position had underscored.

"You forget, Ivor," Ione said, her lips compressed, "that our niece is a woman, not a child. She will make her own decisions." She turned to Margo, smiling. "Yes, dear, Bahira. Didn't you say she worked at the Grand Palm?"

"Oh. No. What I mean is, no, she won't be with us. But yes, she does work here, though she's been so busy I've hardly seen her." Bahira Massoud had been her best friend at Cornell, where they'd both been undergraduates. Bahira had gone on to graduate school in California. It'd been an unlooked-for delight to discover her friend working at the Grand Palm Inn when she'd arrived with her uncle and aunt. "I'm having breakfast with Bahira tomorrow." Tonight she'd be with Cas . . . unless he couldn't get out of his own plans.

"That's nice," Ione said.

Ivor stared at both wife and niece, then shook his head. "Come along, ladies," he said testily, running a practiced eye over their garb. "You both look beautiful. That turquoise satin suit is lovely on you, Margo. Your eyes are like sapphires." He kissed his wife's cheek. "And you look luminescent in that peach silk, my dear."

Niece and aunt exchanged smiles. Ivor had always delighted in what they wore. He doted on them, sometimes too much.

He shut the door behind them and carefully locked it, then followed them into the elevator that sped them to the ground floor. "We'll be eating on the Palm Terrace. We'll have a view of the lagoon and the lights of Disney World," Ivor said, satisfaction in his voice as he ushered them from the elevator and out a door to a flower-edged path that led to another building.

Margo sighed as she walked next to her aunt. She had a fight on her hands. The thought made her queasy. But no matter what, she was not going to have supper with her uncle and his friends. Cas had been magic and she wanted more. They entered the large dining room filled with laughing people, and Margo took a deep breath to gather courage.

"Ah, there they are." Ivor took an arm of each woman and hurried them to where a bar had been set up on the terrace. "Weldon, Celia, how are you? You know my wife, of course. And this is my niece, Mary Gottfriede. We call her Margo."

"So do I."

Even as Margo grasped Mrs. Weldon's hand, the softly spoken words made her turn her head as though in slow motion. Cas! What was he doing there? Were his friends meeting on the terrace too?

"Let go of her, Mother." Cas eased her away from the older woman and bent to kiss her gently.

"That's our son," Weldon Griffith said faintly, eyeing Cas askance.

"Usually he doesn't do that right away," Celia said, goggle-eyed.

"I should hope not," Ivor blustered. "Ahem, Margo. Didn't you say you had another engagement?"

Ione's chuckle built into a full-blown laugh. "I love it. Hoist by your own petard, husband."

"Ione!" Ivor was incensed. "Margo!"

Margo heard the voice from a long way off. She moved her mouth a centimeter from Cas's. "I'm coming, Uncle."

"You're right here. So am I. What's going on? Do you know Weldon and Celia's son?"

"I guess so," Margo said dreamily. "Hi."

"Hi." Cas was out of breath, dizzy. This was the woman his parents wanted him to meet? Damn. His parents had been upset by his adamant refusal to dine with them, but they hadn't argued. He'd been making his own decisions too long. He had conceded the cocktail hour. "I still want to have dinner alone with you," he whispered to Margo, his lips against her ear.

For a moment Margo was hopeful. She wanted to be with Cas so badly. Then she shook her head when she caught sight of the expression of deep disappointment on her uncle's face. "We'd better not."

For a second Cas debated sweeping her up in his arms and running out of the Grand Palm Inn. Then he nodded, kissing her again. He'd promised himself he wouldn't pressure her. He'd go along with the dinner. He intended to see her every chance he could, alone or with others. The kiss went on and on. . . . Cas's heart thudded against his breastbone. He pulled her more fully into his embrace.

"For heaven's sake, Cas, do come up for air," his mother said tartly, her own lips quivering as Ione's amusement increased.

Cas lifted his head, staring at his mother as though she were a stranger. "Hello, Mother. I'm very attracted to Margo."

"Surprise, surprise," Ione said, her mirth turning to glee. She studied her red-faced, glassy-eyed niece. "I think the feeling's mutual." She grinned at her spouse. "Nice going."

Ivor almost dropped his glass.

Weldon took a hefty swallow of his manhattan and choked.

Celia bit her lip. "Heavens."

"We went sailing together," Margo said, out of breath, glaring at Cas. Did he have to be so intense? Uncle Ivor was gasping like a fish out of water. "We'd like to see more of each other."

"Good idea," Ione said.

Cas looked at Ione admiringly. "I like your aunt, darling."

"So do I . . . most of the time," Margo said uneasily. "Ione," she whispered, "Uncle Ivor is getting red."

"I know, I know. This is delicious. I don't know when I've had such a good time."

"Dammit, Ione! I want to know what's going on here. Margo, when did you meet Lancaster?"

Ione put her hands through Weldon's and Celia's arms, urging them toward the French doors to the dining room.

"Lancaster?" Margo murmured to Cas. "How imposing."

"Mary Gottfriede sounds downright regal." He smiled at her. "I didn't expect this."

"Neither did I." She glanced at her uncle, then

back at Cas. "Go slower. My uncle has suffered a shock."

Cas kissed her ear. "I don't know why. They wanted us to meet and like each other. We did meet. And I like you a great deal, Margo. And I think you feel the same." He lifted her chin, smiling when she nodded. To think he might have missed meeting Margo. The thought of skiing in the wilds of Aspen, in all that cold and discomfort, almost made him shudder.

"I don't think Uncle Ivor expected *this*," Margo said. Neither had she. But now it seemed so right.

"We were good together today. Isn't it up to us?" He didn't realize he'd been holding his breath until she nodded.

"Yes." Margo felt as though she'd jumped into the Grand Canyon. "It's up to us. I know nothing about you. You're just as much in the dark about me." Still, she wanted him beside her. She'd felt bereft when she'd been without him for a few hours that afternoon.

"Like you, I know everything and nothing." He'd never let her out of his life . . . unless she told him she hated him.

"Let's go into dinner," Ivor finally said, sounding confused and uncertain.

"Yes, let's," Ione said eagerly. She alone of the four was enthusiastic. "I'm looking forward to this."

"Ione!" Ivor's booming voice turned heads. He frowned at those uncivilized enough to look at him, then took his wife's arm and trolled her into the dining room.

"What's going on, Celia?" Weldon asked his wife as they followed Ivor and Ione. "Do you think the pressure of work has gotten to Cas?"

Celia bit her lower lip and shook her head. "I have no idea."

"It's pressure all right," Ione said gleefully over her shoulder. "But it isn't work related, I'll bet. Ouch, Ivor, you're pinching."

Neither Margo nor Cas heard the exchange. They were completely enraptured with each other.

Two

Margo Tyssen Griffith opened her eyes. What bed-room was this? she wondered. The hotel in Swit-zerland? There'd been so many different ones during their six-week honeymoon, she wasn't always sure where she was. It was like being on a roller-coaster ride. They'd pause on the crest, then rocket downward again. It had been that way from the beginning.

The never ending round of parties, showers, teas, and receptions the two months preceding their marriage had been dizzying. Often her schedule of "events" had been so full, she'd had scant time for the man she loved. The French designer Charine had whipped up her white tis-sue silk dress, a beauty and an original, cut to camouflage the excess weight partying had added to her frame. She'd have gladly given up the dress and all the accoutrements, though, for a little more time with Cas. He was so wildly wonderful.

He'd proposed the first week they were back in town, and they'd married after knowing each other only three months.

She'd been so excited on her wedding day because she'd felt sure all the uncertainties and fears in her life would dissipate when she and Cas were one. Their wedding night had been phenomenal, and the lovemaking was still dynamite. And, she assured herself, all her other alien feelings would fall into place.

Margo rubbed her hand over her rounded middle. Maybe if she had a baby. No. Not yet, not when they didn't know each other. That was silly. Of course they knew each other . . . intimately. Maybe if she dieted. Damn the rich food at those parties, the general all-around cattle calls that had been so much a part of their lives since their first meeting. Even their wedding reception had been like a marathon. It was as though the Fates were preventing them from any sweet, intimate conversation. She loved Cas. She had from the start. Why should she feel uneasy, as though she were living with a stranger. He was her darling, and making love to him was everything.

She felt the warmth at her back and sighed. Cas was there. She was getting used to waking up with him. When the arm around her waist tightened, she smiled and turned, her eyes closing. This was the best part. Lovemaking was the great communicator. She wanted her husband with a hunger that shook her. It flashed through her mind that they should have better understanding on other levels than they did. But she swept away the errant thought. It had intruded too many times. She wouldn't deal with it now.

"Umm, you smell good." Cas, sleepy eyed, pressed her to him, his mouth touching her eyes, her cheeks. "I should shave, brush my teeth," he mumbled.

"So should I," she said, tightening her arms around him. It felt so good to hold him. Sometimes, it was as though what they had could slip away. Why did it seem so elusive when it was so hot? Could strangers dwell in a torrid, wild relationship and still be strangers?

Cas let his mouth slide down her body, seeking the wonder of every pore, loving her skin, her essence. She was so warm and inviting. He needed that. "You have wonderful skin, Margo. And I'm going to kiss all of it."

Passion rippled through her like an oil-eating flame, and Margo hugged him closer. The firm musculature of his body excited her as nothing ever had. She wanted him so badly, it unbalanced her. Only her husband could do that. Lord! Cas could swallow her whole. Margo considered herself easygoing, bordering on indolent. Let the world flow by her, she was a happy spectator, with no real need to be a participant. But at times Cas's power, the ease with which he'd replaced her uncle as chief orchestrator of her life, was like a match to tinder. Annoyance had become common in her life, and the more she tried to hide it from Cas, the more irked she became. The irritation wasn't directed at him, but at herself. She was letting him dominate her life just as Ivor had. Stand up! she told herself. Speak out! Let your feelings be known! No matter how much she lectured herself, though, she'd done nothing. It was so easy to go with the flow.

She leaned toward her husband and kissed his nipples. His body contracted. Her libido climbed.

They faced each other, naked bodies quivering in want.

Cas cupped her buttocks with his hands. "Beautiful." Then he took one breast into his mouth, sucking gently. "I dream of doing this, sweet."

"Then please don't stop," she told him huskily. This was why she was born, to love Cas. If there were uncertainties, they'd be ironed out. Then her thoughts and emotions were flung into the vortex, and she spun into the heat.

Body to body, mouth to mouth, they took each other. Her joyous whimpers, his delighted growls, were an accompaniment to the building tide. Sexual hunger had them in sway.

Her breasts were flattened against him, his chest hair tickling her soft flesh like an airy caress. Breath sobbed from her as she wriggled closer, wanting, needing his touch. When his tongue traveled across her cheek to her ear, she twisted so that he'd be even closer. His teeth worried her tender earlobe. She cried out. His uneven breathing swept her skin, prickling it, making it goose-bump in delight. Her legs rubbed his in urgent response to the heat, wanting more, more.

He stretched her arms above her head, threading his fingers with hers, his thumbs scoring her palms, his lower body whorling against her. He grinned at her, then he kissed her, mouth open, carnal, wanting, holding nothing back. When she freed her hands and dug her fingers into his shoulders, he shook with need. His kisses increased in intensity, his tongue rubbed her into fire. Sliding to the side he cupped her breasts, then licked the distended nipples. Then he took the nipple full into his mouth, sucking, drawing, pulling gently.

Slashes of sunlight spilled across their bodies. Margo could see the harshness of her husband's features as they tightened in passion. His hair and body were a silvery bronze. All of him glinted like an ancient Greek god. Thunderous passion built in her like floodwaters behind a dam. To know it all, feel it all, was the ultimate crescendo. Her hand swiped at the sweat on his face as he smiled down at her.

"You're wet for me, love," he murmured. "But there's more." Sliding down her body, he kissed every inch. At the junction of her legs he kissed the soft black tangle of hair.

On fire, Margo thrashed on the bed, holding him to her as he thrust inside her. Stars and planets exploded behind her eyes. A hot ball of flame consumed her, ecstasy lifting her, casting her further and further.

He took her and gave to her, letting her legs and body imprison him.

Thought left them and they thrust together, clinging, climbing, whirling in the eye of the cyclone. Cleaving the heavens, they flew past the stars. They died together and lived again, all in one momentous splash of time. In the slow downward spiral they were silent. The whole world had been theirs for the eternity of a moment.

After several minutes, Cas moved off her and smiled. "I love your skin. It's luminescent, and you're so damned sultry. Did you escape from a seraglio just to be my love slave? You have a wonderful body, Margo. Do you know that?"

"Yes, you've told me." She stroked his face, loving those hard planes. And she loved having him with her all the time. But sometimes she wished they were home in Manhattan and not traveling all over like Gypsies. Yet Cas seemed to be so happy taking her so many places. Hadn't they seen much of Europe? Now he was talking about China, Japan, India . . . When would they get back to their own lives in the United States?

"Cas," she said hesitantly, "how can you afford to be away from your business for so long? You're in the communications field. Doesn't that make frequent changes and turns?" She caught his quick frown, the closed look.

"Yes, it does. But let me worry about that. I have a good staff. I don't want you to worry about anything."

"Of course." She pulled his head down to her, loving his touch, needing it, hating the needles of uncertainty.

After kissing her, he leaned back, his smile quizzical. "What are you thinking?"

"That this is wonderful." He was always first out of their sexual aura, the first lucid one to find the way back to earth. She wanted to tell him she loved him, but she held back, as always. It was a high wall she was leery of climbing. Cas was reserved now, far more so than he'd been at their first meeting.

Love. They'd never used that word between them. It was silly of her to fret. Their life was good, they didn't need words to define it. Maybe it was better to never use binding words such as *love*. So many of their friends and acquaintances "loved" everything, especially their spouses. Some of them were in the process of divorcing or had been divorced. Some had severed their "love forever" relationships. Yes, indeed, it could be better never to use that four-letter word.

Cas touched her. "You seem so far away."

Margo studied his handsome face. His eyes were unreadable. Had he noticed her reticence? If only he'd talk about his feelings, maybe then she could open up with him. Or would he become more like Uncle Ivor? Overriding every objection, taking every jump for her, quite sure he knew what was best. Had she exchanged one sweet yoke for another? That was her own fault. She should speak out, tell Cas and her uncle how she felt.

Stifling a sigh, she smiled at him. "I was just ruminating. We had a wonderful wedding, didn't we?"

His palpable pause, and that twist of smile, said he knew she vacillated. She opened her mouth to tell him she was wildly in love with him, that she needed him mind, body, and soul. The words died aborning. They had not used words after the first day. It'd been touches, kisses, embraces, love-giving that spoke for them. Those first days they'd known each other had been crucial, and they'd colored the future. If only they'd been able to proceed on their own, not with other people and the constant interference, however well meaning, that had come with it. Maybe if he'd not met her uncle, not known how fragile she was, how cosseted. If they'd had those four days alone in Florida, perhaps they might have opened up with each other so much, there'd have been no room for fences between them. She ached to tell him how she felt, yet she was loath to destroy the delicate balance of oneness they'd already attained . . . in bed, in silence. Her body told him openly, as his told her, but the words remained hidden. When they faced each other in the clear light of day, the fences appeared. It was silly. He ran a billion-dollar communications business with astounding panache, according to Uncle Ivor. She, with her education and exposure to high-strata social life, knew how to deal with a variety of people. But with each other they spoke through sex. Even now her body was reacting just because his one finger traveled down her side.

Cas leaned down and kissed her cheek. "What would you think about traveling to Nepal to ski?"

"Nepal?" They wouldn't be going home. She swallowed her disappointment and smiled at him. "Almost to China. What a distance." At least she'd be with Cas. And they'd go home soon.

He nodded. "My contacts tell me the skiing is excellent. Much of the powder is virgin, and now there are some very modern facilities we can use. And you do like to ski." His smile touched her like a brand. "I like making you happy, Margo, taking you to places you've never been. We'll be at home for years. Right?"

"Right." When he smiled like that, her heart

turned over. Of course he was right. They should be doing wonderful things together. They'd be home soon. Home! Beginning their life together . . . No! She was being childish. Better to take advantage of the wonderful opportunity to travel. Besides, Cas was so eager to go.

"Hey!" he said, kissing her nose. "You do like to ski, and you'd like to go, wouldn't you?"

Once more, Margo gave in. "Very much. I think it would be wonderful to ski in Nepal. What an adventure."

Cas grinned. "I aim to please, Mrs. Griffith."

"I guess we're lucky you have such an able staff and can be away so long."

"Right." He kissed her chin. "I'll make the arrangements."

The days flew by until they left Switzerland. They skied and went sight-seeing and shopped in the wonderful but expensive chocolate shops, sweater boutiques, ski barns. They also managed to meet two other people, Kurt and Suzy Lutz, who were ski aficionados. When Cas mentioned the trip to Nepal, the Lutzes enthusiastically agreed to join them.

Cas and Margo were packed and ready to leave the hotel for the airport when the telephone rang. Cas picked it up impatiently.

"Yes? . . . What? When? . . . Dammit all, why didn't you watch it? That contract is important and not just monetarily. The prestige doesn't hurt one bit. Now that we've moved into the cinematic field, we have to walk on eggs. We don't need trouble. . . . I know. Well, can you call my father? . . . He didn't have any luck?"

Margo watched the varying emotions stream across Cas's face. Incredulity, anger, finally acceptance. He slammed down the phone and turned to her. "I'll have to go back to New York. For two days, no more, I promise, Margo."

She reached out and touched his arm. "There's a problem, obviously. Let's cancel the trip. We'll go back together."

He hesitated, then shook his head. "No way. The weather is perfect in Nepal and we're going to ski there. The only difference is, you're going direct. I'm doing the triangle. But I'll be there before you miss me, sweetheart." He kissed her deeply, his pulse pounding when she swayed against him. "We've never been parted," he whispered against her mouth.

"Then let me go with you," she said, feeling teary.

"No," he said hoarsely. "You've looked forward to this. Suzy and Kurt will be with you. I don't want you to miss a day of it."

"They're people we met. We're on our honeymoon, aren't we?" She stepped closer, loving the feel of power that passion brought.

Cas laughed. "We've been on one for six weeks." He kissed her forehead. "But you like the Lutzes, just as I do. And they're the first new friends we've shared."

She nodded. "That does make them special, but . . ."

She argued further for accompanying him, but Cas was adamant, so she smiled and agreed. She was proud of the way she hid her heavy heart. Parting from him was agony.

Cas kissed her over and over again, passionately when they separated at the airport. He waited just inside the terminal until her plane was aloft and out of sight. Then he ran to where a plane was waiting at the gate for him. In minutes he was on his way back to the United States.

Margo talked with Suzy and Kurt desultorily, hoping she responded and smiled at the proper times. She read and slept. When a tray was put in front of her, she teased the food with her fork. She felt so empty, so lost, without Cas. Each mile that separated her from him was like a knife wound. She loved him and she wanted to scream it to the clouds scudding past the window.

The flight was a long one, but the congenial attendants, the wide choice of movies, and the ability to move about in the wide aisle made it bearable. At their first stop, Bombay, Margo had the sensation of being disembodied when she walked off the plane after being so long in the air.

"I wish we were staying overnight and then flying to Nepal," Suzy said plaintively. "I'd like to regain my land legs."

Margo nodded.

"Nonsense, ladies," Kurt said bracingly. "Once we're on that plane and heading toward the Himalayas, you'll be glad we went at once. We won't miss a day of skiing."

Margo smiled, even as she thought, *the hell with skiing!* She wanted Cas and their new life at home. So what if some of it might be humdrum? Cas was in her life, and down through the years their reticence with each other would change. They'd talk and laugh and all would be well.

There was a short time between planes. Soon they were airborne again in a much smaller jet. And how the topography changed. Margo was sure they could touch some of the peaks they passed over. They were not far from Katmandu when it began to snow. Thick, heavy flakes coated the small windows, and even the highest peaks were camouflaged in white.

The pilot announced that the weather ahead was worsening and he was going to find an alternate field where he could land until the weather changed.

"He seems to be flying far to the north," Kurt said.

Margo couldn't tell, but she assumed all was well.

When the engine coughed and they banked sharply, she ignored the gasps and murmurs of the few other passengers. Nothing would happen. Cas was going to join her in a few days. They'd be together.

Then the plane shuddered violently, as though the craft were being buffeted by giant hands.

"We're going down," Kurt said in shock, grasping his wife.

Margo grabbed the pillow she'd used and put it behind her neck and another on her knees as the attendants gave quick instructions for a crash landing.

The pilot fought the plane down and landed fairly smoothly, though the plane bucked and jerked over the rough terrain. It was when one wing tipped and caught something that they spun around. There was a ripping, crashing sound and the smell of fuel. The lights went out except for those in the aisle. Then they struck something with a rending blast. Fire and blackness and smoke and screaming engulfed Margo.

Margo fought to be free of the black smoke. She couldn't see or breathe. She was choking. Flames were all around her. She dropped to the floor and crawled, trying to recall where the closest exit had been. Then she saw a streak of light. There was an explosion, and she was lifted up and tossed like a ball, banging against hard objects that were burning and now burned her. Then she was whirled through a blast of cold air. She tried to call out, but she couldn't. She was freezing, but she was glad because it stopped the burning. She struck something and knew no more.

Once she woke and knew she was blind. She could see nothing and was so cold, she could feel nothing. She remembered Suzy and Kurt, but she didn't know where they were. Then there was merciful blackness again. She didn't waken or make a sound when four monks found her. They wrapped her in yak skins, and put her on the sled they'd pulled.

Three

January 1991

The ocean and sky had the same steely look. The plane carrying Margo Tyssen Griffith, now calling herself T'ang Qi, knifed its way above the scattered clouds on its trip from London to New York.

Margo had been brought back from the jaws of death. She could almost laugh at the analogy if it hadn't been so true. Now, she was going home not quite two years after she'd left Switzerland for Nepal. It was all such a fantasy. Even with the last of the plastic surgery behind her and only a barely visible facial scar, she could hardly believe what had happened. That she would've died had not the monks found her, she knew. That she'd hovered between life and death as weeks dragged into months was a fact. That she'd been bedridden for five months, fighting to stay alive, she accepted. But the rest . . . it was unreal. She sighed, staring out at the clouds hanging heavy and gray, the sun's rays streaking across their tops, and as always, thought of Cas. Had he heard of the painter and sculptor T'ang Qi? Could he ever guess that it was his wife Margo? Never. Would he accept her? Uncertainties and fears crowded in on her, and she murmured her mantra to gain serenity. She would deal with one moment, one hour, one day, at a time.

Lhasa, Tibet, was behind her, as was her old self. She was changed inside and out, slimmed down to seeming fragility from the lingering effects of her injuries. But she was well, and mostly because of her mentor. She'd clung to T'ang as an anchor to life. He'd listened to her feverish ravings, later to her frustrated murmurings as an invalid, and finally to her conversations. He was her dear friend who knew her inside and out. She'd even revealed her secret desire to be a painter and sculptor. While she was still recovering, fighting every moment against the pain, T'ang had encouraged her to use her talents in painting and sculpting as part of her therapy. He'd counseled and supported her as she was brought back to full health by *qi cong*, an ancient Chinese method of healing. She could still hear his voice urging her on, admonishing her never to waste her life or her abilities. And he'd been the one who told her, after the time of healing was over, that she would have her final cosmetic surgery in London. Now it was finished and she was flying back to Cas. Cas! He didn't know she was alive. She hated the fear—fear of flying, fear of landing . . . fear of seeing her husband. Yet, she had to see him. Courage! She wouldn't crash this time!

Only painting and sculpting had kept her sane these last two months, and she'd worked like a demon in London, just as she had at the lamasery, turning out piece after piece. Once she'd devoted herself to art, her life had expanded to new levels, new horizons. From the very beginning she'd worked furiously in both media, as though she had to catch up with the lost years of doing nothing with her talent. Though she'd chafed at her slow recovery, longing to be reunited with her husband, she'd reveled in learning. When she'd been strong enough to contact him, she couldn't face doing it through another party or by phoning him. The thought of trying to convince him who she was over the phone nauseated her. It wouldn't be easy facing him, but that was the only way to do it, head-on, open, nothing hidden. But what if he was married? What if he didn't want her? She inhaled against the pain, closing her eyes for a moment. She would have to handle whatever came along.

Now she could speak a passable Mandarin and Tibetan. She'd dealt with herself and her insecurities, becoming assured, confident. She'd all but read her way through the library kept by the monks, mostly the English works, but she'd faltered through some French and German too. And when she was on her feet, she'd begun her lessons in t'ai chi, the martial art akin to *qi cong*. Her body, mind, and spirit had responded, and she'd found a serenity she hadn't dreamed existed. With her mentor's permission she'd put aside her own name and adopted his, becoming T'ang Qi. Now whatever faced her, no matter how unpalatable, she'd take care of it. After all, she had her work.

One of the monks who was in contact with the outside world had taken a few of her works to Lhasa. They'd been snapped up by the agent of a wealthy Japanese businessman who had a private collection worth millions. The agent had demanded all she had. Even before she left the lamasery for her final surgery in London, she'd become known to a select few art collectors, earning substantial sums for her works. All those months of confinement when she'd worked to gain serenity, when the volume of her works just grew, had begun to pay off as a career. It was as though her brush with death and her racking recovery had released a wellspring of talent in her. Her previous attempts in college seemed pallid by comparison. Everything in her life had changed—except her flaming need to get back to her husband. Just the previous week, after she'd recovered from her surgery, she'd had a one-woman show in London. Though much of her work had been purchased by her Japanese sponsor, there'd been many inquiries about the rest. Her star was rising in the art world.

Compulsively, Margo touched the faint scar on her cheek. What would Cas say about it? Would he think her different? Her looks were changed. T'ang had told her she looked like a fragile Chinese flower. She'd lost many pounds, revealing her delicate bone structure. Her hair, always jet black and curly, was now the same black but cropped short and sleek, capping her head and combed forward to emphasize her now-prominent cheekbones. She wore cheongsams now, slim-fitting silk dresses, mostly for comfort. And on her feet, she rarely wore anything but flat shoes. Except for her dark blue eyes and creamy skin tones, she could be oriental.

The plane banked into a new heading. Margo looked out the window. The Statue of Liberty! Strikingly beautiful. Had she ever looked at it before? The plane banked again, and then New York was spread out beneath her.

It looked vastly different, yet painfully the same. Tall buildings speared the sky in uneven marches across the island of Manhattan, glittering jewel-like in the sun. Clouds puffed the blue sky back-drop. The crisscrossing streets were dotted with vehicles. Soon she would be back there among them.

Margo inhaled deeply and smiled at the flight attendant, who reminded her to fasten her seat belt. Had she ever looked at the city before? Margo relaxed and watched lazily as the jumbo jet touched down, then screamed along the runway, slowing as the terminal came into view. Home! Cas!

Licking her lips, she murmured the prayers her mentor had taught her about serenity and strength. Now she was T'ang Qi, the artist, and her works had been shown. The unsold portion of her collection would be shown in New York tomorrow. She feared nothing, not failure, not rejection. She'd come to terms with herself and her world through the wisdom of her mentor and her own increasing confidence. Then her husband's face appeared before her, and for a second her courage failed her. If he had remarried . . . Her chin went up a notch. That was beyond her control. Only her destiny and the seeking of it was within her grasp. The rest was in the hands of the Fates. Whatever happened, Confucius said, the river would go on.

She rose to her feet, moving rhythmically, her body conditioned and supple by hours of physical, mental, and spiritual training. The London doctors had pronounced her in great shape. She strode toward the exit of the plane, bowing slightly to the captain and the flight attendants nearby. Her murmured thanks were received with smiles.

Surrounded suddenly by the noise in the Kennedy terminal, she paused, blinking. She muttered her mantra and inner peace was hers again. After passing quickly through customs—showing the Japanese passport her sponsor had acquired for her—she entered a large waiting area. Someone called her name, and she turned to see a uniformed chauffeur approaching her. He'd been hired by her sponsor, he told her as he took her luggage.

"Thank you," she said, and gladly followed him out of the hubbub and confusion of Kennedy Airport. There were so many people. All strangers? Would she be recognized? Probably not.

She had been jolted badly when her mentor had told her that a body had been identified as hers. The lamas hadn't known who she was until she'd completely woken from her semicomatose state, many weeks after the bodies of the other passengers on the plane, all dead, had been retrieved as well as possible and the incident all but forgotten by the papers. Margo often wondered who the woman was who'd been misidentified as herself.

Outside the terminal building, the driver led her to a black limousine. As he pulled away from the curb, he glanced in the rearview mirror at her. "I understand you're from China, Miss T'ang," he said, smiling.

Margo smiled back. He was an older man, rather distinguished. "Tibet, actually."

"My son owns this car and three others," the man said proudly. "I'm retired, but I help out." He glanced over his shoulder at her. "I flew the Hump in World War Two. I like that part of the world. Nice people."

"Very." Margo felt a warm glow. She'd forgotten how friendly New Yorkers could be. How much more could she have forgotten in the past two years? Was she misremembering the powerful love she'd felt for Cas? No! If anything, she loved him more than when they'd parted in Switzerland, for now she was better able to love.

"You're staying at the Plaza, Miss T'ang?" the driver asked.

"Yes." Margo smiled to herself. She'd never stayed in a hotel in Manhattan. Before she'd married Cas, she'd had a condominium on Riverside Drive. She supposed it had been sold.

"I'll have you there in no time, miss. By the way, my name's Carbo." The driver smiled at her again, then raised the window between them.

Margo gazed out at the flood of traffic, wondering at the pell-mell thrust of people and vehicles. Once it had seemed so natural. Perhaps it still was, but she'd learned other ways that had given her life deeper meaning, and she would never forget that. Would Cas allow her to show him the wonders she'd discovered? She would always be grateful for the chance to regroup and recapture her life—although there would forever be an empty space in it if Cas did not take her back.

They soon arrived at the Plaza Hotel. Carbo carried her bags in for her, and she asked him to pick her up the next day at noon to take her to the gallery. The opening show would be in the evening, but she needed to check the arrangement of her paintings and sculptures.

With a minimum of fuss she verified her reservation and was shown to her spacious room. As she paced its length, she wondered where Cas was, what he was doing at that moment. She stared at the phone, then shook her head. After dining in her room on a small salad and brown rice, she did her ritualistic exercises and went to bed. Despite her jet lag, it took all of her concentration to wipe her mind clean of its turmoil. At last she fell asleep.

The next day she breakfasted on juice, barley biscuit, and tea. After going to the gallery, she decided, she'd have Carbo drive her to Cas's office. She'd wait until he was free to see her, no matter how long that was.

Carbo picked her up exactly at noon. During the short drive to the Madison Avenue gallery, she concentrated on her mantra and murmured her prayers. This was her first outing in her own country. Carbo was able to stop directly in front of the gallery. As he helped her to the sidewalk, she told him she'd call him when she was ready to leave.

She stood in front of the gallery and gazed at it as the limousine pulled away. The sun speckled the granite facade so that it flashed jewellike. The winter air was crisp, reminding her of the clean Tibetan air. She was so engrossed in her thoughts, she didn't notice the person at her elbow until he spoke.

"Give me your purse and don't make no fuss, lady. I gotta knife."

"In the middle of the day? Heavens," she murmured.

Margo looked into the man's eyes. Fear. Emptiness. Desperation. He could hurt someone. That didn't shock her. What did shock her was another man running toward them. Cas! Determined, grim faced . . . *Oh, Lord!* she thought. He had sized up the situation and was going to intervene. In that flash of time she also realized Cas hadn't recognized her. Nor could he see the knife the man held.

Lightning fear gave impetus to smooth action. She dropped her shoulders, wiped her mind clean, murmured the ancient words, and her body became a machine. Faster than the eye could follow, her one leg came around like a scythe as her arms rose in the defensive position. Leg and one arm struck the man like falling timbers. His jaw cracked from the blow of her forearm; her leg immobilized his lower body as it sent paralyzing messages to his spine. With barely a cry he was on the ground, writhing. Then Cas was lifting him up and shaking him like a rag doll, the look of violence on his face stunning Margo, rooting her to the sidewalk.

"You son of a . . ." Cas pulled back his arm, his fist closed tightly, his teeth bared.

"No!" Margo touched his arm. "Defense is one thing. To maim a man does you no credit. Violence is not the answer to violence."

Shocked, Cas turned toward her, his grip lessening. *That voice!* he thought. The image of his wife jumped into his mind. Groaning inaudibly, he shook his head, trying to clear it of the whispers that had plagued him for almost two years.

Feeling the grip on him lessen, the attacker wriggled away, rolled to his feet, and ran, favoring one leg, one hand covering his jaw.

"Damn!" Cas swung around and looked after the man, his hands closing and opening. "We'll never catch him now."

"He's already caught in a web of his own making," Margo said softly. She turned toward the gallery, every thread of serenity in her body threatened, nerve endings twanging like too taut guitar strings. Cas was unnaturally pale. He looked hollow eyed, grittily unhappy. She'd wanted him so long. Now he was in front of her. She took deep breaths to calm herself.

"You're T'ang Qi, aren't you?" Cas asked. She was the same height as Margo, he mused, but she didn't have his wife's wonderfully curving body. She was slender, almost fragile, but there was a strength to her too. He'd seen how she'd taken the thief down. Of course, she was oriental

. . . but there was some occidental in her. Those eyes, that skin. Her face was a different shape from Margo's, yet there was something familiar. Damn! He was going crazy. He still saw Margo everywhere.

Margo paused, glancing back to look at him. That was a mistake. Her heart rose in her throat. He was still beautiful. But there was a worn-out look to him . . . and a smell of alcohol and tobacco. He was hollow cheeked, and though his eyes were the same emerald green, they were now red rimmed, as though he slept intermittently or not well. His clothes didn't fit as if they'd been poured on him as they once did. They hung on him. Smooth, svelte, sophisticated Cas Griffith had a baggy look!

"Yes," she answered, "I'm T'ang Qi." Afraid her voice would break if she said more, she walked toward the gallery.

She was intercepted by a man racing out of the building.

"Are you all right, Miss T'ang? I saw what happened from my office window. I'm Charles Verdon. I supervise Mackay Galleries. The man who attacked you . . ."

"You won't catch him," Cas said testily. "You're too late."

Margo glanced at him in surprise. She never recalled his being so cutting, so short with people, as though he could barely tolerate their company. His annoyance was understandable; someone could have gotten hurt. It was not Charles Verdon's fault, but Cas was acting as though it was. When had he become a bear?

She allowed Charles Verdon to escort her into the gallery and was startled when Cas followed them. Mr. Verdon seemed to know him. What was he doing there?

"That was quite a defensive play you made," Cas drawled in her ear as he helped her take her coat off. "T'ai chi?"

"Yes," she said, surprised that he knew it. And surprised, too, at the acid twist to his voice. He sounded so . . . cynical.

"How long will you be staying in the country?" Cas didn't realize he'd been holding his breath until she shrugged. He exhaled heavily. "So, your plans are up in the air?"

"Yes, I suppose you could say that."

She must be used to Western ways, he thought. She hadn't even questioned the colloquialism he'd used. He inhaled her essence. The body fragrance was new to him . . . but there was a familiarity. Not for a long time had a woman so intrigued him. He wanted her. "Perhaps you'll give me a personal tour of the gallery and tell me about your works."

"I think they speak for themselves," she said quietly, though her heart thudded out of rhythm. Cas was by her side! Her body and mind ballooned with joy.

Staring down at her, Cas was suddenly glad that his mother had insisted he check on how things were going for this first American show of the art world's newest sensation. Proceeds from the tickets to that night's opening cocktail party would go to Celia Griffith's favorite charity for abused and homeless children. Remembering how his mother practically had to beg him that morning to stop by the gallery, Cas laughed.

Margo glanced at him questioningly. "Something is funny?"

"I'm laughing at my own fancies and fantasies," he answered. And he was more than willing to spin one around her. What did it matter that she reminded him so forcefully of Margo? Hell, the last two years, even a curbstone could've done that. He'd only been able to get his wife out of his mind for minutes at a stretch. That had to change. Time to get a new canvas, or at least try. And he was looking at one he'd like to color himself into, fast. Did Orientals ever have such blue eyes? Or were they black? Or green? He'd never seen their like, except . . . No. Don't think of Margo. Obviously she had occidental blood. The combination of East and West was wild and beautiful.

For the past two years he'd exerted an iron control over himself. He'd had to, or lose his mind. With Margo gone he'd put all his energies into his work, and he'd made pots of money, more than he'd ever spend. He'd manipulated his expanding communications business like a ventriloquist his dummy, and it had given him a small measure of satisfaction in his agony of loss. Along with the fierce business drive had come a monumental self-control that had stood him good stead in a myriad of situations. But now that control was being undermined by a slip of a woman he didn't know. The women who'd streamed through his life since Margo's death had all been highly motivated and intelligent . . . and not interested in long commitments. It had worked for him, until now. A strange impatience coursed through him, and a lacing of fear. He didn't like the sensation. He felt like an unfledged boy, hands and feet flapping, trying to gain a toehold. On what? How had this artist managed to unglue him when he'd been welded so tight?

He watched as she crossed the gallery with Verdon, examining her various large canvases hanging on the walls, and the sculptures artistically arranged around the room. Despite that air of fragility about her, she moved with the latent energy of a tiger. What was it about her that so intrigued him? She was sexually perfect. He didn't know how he knew that, but he did. He wanted her . . . yet she made him feel clumsy. He shifted his shoulders as though his tailor-made suit coat fit too tightly, as though he could toss off the strange sensations she engendered in him. He hurried after her.

"Aren't you going to show me your works?" he asked.

"Aren't you coming to the opening, Mr. Griffith?" she countered.

"Yes." He stared at her. The way she said his name made him shiver with a certainty that he knew her. "Have we ever met, Miss T'ang?"

"In this life or another?" Margo laughed lowly, though her heart skipped a beat. Had he recognized her? Well, it didn't matter. She would soon tell him who she was, but this wasn't the place for intimate disclosure. And after she told him, she would see Uncle Ivor and Aunt Ione. It all sounded easy, but she was well aware it could explode in her face.

Margo muttered her mantra. What a strange world it was. She'd been going to contact Cas that afternoon. It had all been fixed in her mind. She'd never guessed he'd be here. But then she'd never discovered his taste in art when they were married. When had they discussed likes and dislikes? There'd been so many closed doors. Sometimes when she thought of her marriage, it had an unreal quality, as though it had been a dream.

She smiled fleetingly at him, then turned away as Charles gestured toward another of her paintings.

Watching her walk away from him, Cas made a sudden decision. He peremptorily strode into Verdon's office and called his personal assistant, Ernest Delwain. He nearly gave the man a stroke when he told him to cancel all of that day's appointments.

"But, sir," Ernest protested, "you've been working night and day on the Belasceau—"

"Put it off. I'll call you tomorrow."

Cas slammed down the phone and hurried back into the main showroom. Not since Margo died had he felt such a sense of tingling urgency, of need. He quieted the usual quiver of pain at the thought of his wife. He had to put the agonizing frustrations behind him. There was no way he could bring Margo back and start again, no matter how many times he dreamed he could. Right after her death he'd entertained the thought of following her, but he'd fought off the futility of that and buried himself in work. He was coming back, slowly, to the real world. He was better, he was sure of it, despite the skepticism of family and friends. And nothing had proved that to him more than the appearance of T'ang Qi that very day. In fact, he was certain he was on a new threshold, a brand-new beginning to life. Damn! He'd have to tell his mother he owed her one for this day. Grinning, something he hadn't done for two years, he hustled after T'ang Qi.

She was standing with Verdon and two gallery assistants, discussing one of her paintings. Cas stood directly behind her. His blood thudded in want, surprising him. When he stared at the hint of round bottom barely camouflaged by her cheongsam, his hands itched to cup the luscious flesh. She was beautifully sexy, and her legs were gorgeous. His body heated as he studied T'ang Qi. He was used to sexual heat when with an attractive woman, and he was adept at making moves on them. He enjoyed it. But this was different. It was more than just desire. He wanted to know the inside of T'ang Qi. That hadn't happened in so long. Out of the blue he remembered his first meeting with Margo on the Seven Seas Lagoon, of falling in the water, and how she'd later accused him of pushing her in to even the score. And he chuckled. Amazing! Usually recalling anything about Margo brought pain.

Margo stiffened, feeling him behind her, his breath on her hair, his low laugh so familiar, so hot, so brand-new, so enticing. Her body melted with desire. All those months in Tibet she'd felt little or no sexual passion. Her focus was elsewhere. Delight for her had been to overcome

T'ang in one of the many intricate moves of t'ai chi, or chess. Now, back in Manhattan, all the pent-up desire for Cas flooded through her, obliterating all the reserves and barriers she'd erected during her long convalescence. And she knew, with a swamping certainty, that he was all of life to her, and her being would be gray without him. She could have turned at that moment and torn the clothes from his back, made mad, impassioned love to him on the floor of the gallery, and said to hell with the world. The torridness of it had her gasping.

Charles Verdon turned to her. "Did you say something, Miss T'ang?"

"No." But he was there, behind her, his breath like a torch to her skin.

"Did too," Cas whispered in her ear.

Margo bit her lip, mirth rolling up, up into her throat. She needed her mentor at that moment to force her to repeat her mantra, to bring herself under control. Heavens, she was losing her dignity. She couldn't get hysterical in the art gallery. Yet, she had the strongest urge to turn around and stick out her tongue at Lancaster McCross Griffith. Biting her lip harder, she stared at the work in front of her.

"As I said," she managed, "I've titled this *Ascendancy.* I was just coming out of a rather bleak period in my life, realizing that I was going to survive, that my life would change for the better."

"Mine's changing too," Cas said, standing so close to her that his whisper was inaudible to the others. The curve of her buttock almost touched his thigh. Hot tension spread through him in waves, hardening his body. It shocked him to have such a reaction. Not since . . . No! He'd begun a new way of thinking. No more going back.

Knowing that he was following her charged Margo, like putting a plug into a socket. Power was roaring through her, heat, light, explosive new energies. It had been like that the first time she'd met him. They'd been open with each other in those first precious hours. Eons ago. She blinked to put the past behind her. Words poured out of her about her work, the input of her mentor, the lasting impressions of the Chinese masters of sculpture and calligraphy, the serenity of the words of Confucius that permeated her life.

Then the informal tour was over and she'd visited every piece of work on display, and that included the sold pieces from the London show. The show would remain intact until the end of the tour. Whatever wasn't sold would be returned to her. Out of the corner of her eye she saw Cas jotting down something on a piece of paper that he handed to Charles, who then stared at him, mouth agape.

When Cas noticed she was watching him, he grinned, then strolled toward her. "I bought your works."

"Oh? How nice. Which did you buy?"

"All but the ones that were sold in London. If those owners back out, I have an option on them too. Oops, your mouth is hanging open. I wonder what your public would think of that."

"You're insane. That's a fortune."

"I've amassed more than one fortune in the last

two years." He smiled bitterly. "I can afford to spend one." What would she say if he told her that he'd scarcely been able to sleep in two years, that when he wasn't out carousing all night, he was gambling at the highest level with his own money? What he'd wanted to do in the beginning was lose everything, destroy himself. When it didn't work that way, when he began to show a huge profit, he'd started calculating his risks and forgetting about losses. He hadn't planned to branch out into real estate and stocks and bonds. Communications was his field. But when his wild gambling into unknown markets had paid off, he'd begun to take them seriously. When disreputable real estate was considered a goner, he'd purchased blocks and turned them into money-makers.

"I'd like to show you some of the things I've done," he said. "They're not art, but they have a style." His eagerness to show his "works" to her surprised him. He hadn't given a damn about anyone's opinion in so long.

"Tell me about them." She was thirsting to hear of all of his endeavors, day by day, minute by minute.

"Well, one of my particular favorites is the mooring on the East River for a flotilla of floating restaurants." His father had almost had a stroke when he'd begun that venture, but it too had proved profitable.

Margo was taken aback by that. Cas had always been successful . . . but in communications. "Sounds fashionable."

A bell went off in his head at the very Western remark. He had that sense of familiarity again.

"And it pays its way." It had netted him millions when he'd sold out. What would she say if he told her that his own father had been frightened for him because he sensed a desperation about the way his son made so much money? "Don't worry about getting the money for your art, lovely. The pieces will be paid for tomorrow. And they will be insured for the rest of the tour."

Margo smiled serenely. "Sounds well thought out." Insurance companies too? she mused. Did he work day and night? He didn't exactly look tired. Rather he seemed stripped to the bone, like a too taut wire that twanged with tension. All at once she felt hemmed in, crowded. He'd bought all her paintings! Even not knowing who she was, was he trying to manage her life? She wanted him desperately, all of him, even the black side that she'd never seen until this day. The violence in his face when he'd held the would-be purse snatcher had shocked her. Had it always been there? For a moment she was uneasy. Had she ever known the husband she'd loved so much? Were there more unknown facets of him? Whatever the answers were, she'd deal with them because she loved and wanted him. But she would not surrender her personal autonomy. It had taken a brush with death and a relearning of life to teach her that she must love and give, but also control her own life, seek her own destiny. Only then could she show a perfect love to her husband, because she'd be able to love herself.

Cas saw the infinitesimal tightening of her features. Her eyes seemed to become a bit opaque, as though she needed to exclude him. He sensed that she relished and protected her privacy and would share only what she wished to share. In that way she was unlike Margo, whom he'd been able to read like an open book. Uneasiness made him shift his shoulders. Yet, there'd been times when he'd remembered his brief marriage and wondered if he'd known his wife at all.

Telling himself once more to forget Margo, he concentrated on T'ang Qi. Even with her sudden withdrawal into herself, he felt sure he could learn to know her better than he had Margo. That jolted him. He was a fool. T'ang Qi wasn't like Margo at all. Why was the memory of Margo so intrusive now?

"Will you have dinner with me tonight?" he asked abruptly.

For a moment Margo wanted to run. Then reason asserted itself. What had she returned to the West for? Not for her art, not for money, not for prestige. She'd come back for the love she needed in her life and the only man who could give it to her. "Yes," she answered. "Shall I meet you somewhere?" He hadn't said he was married, she mused. Of course, he thought he was a widower. He didn't wear a ring, not even the one she'd put on his finger when they'd made their vows. Hers had been lost somewhere in Tibet. Yes, she'd go with him. She'd fully intended to find a way to see him. Fate had presented this golden way.

"Why don't I pick you up here?"

"Oh . . . no." The thought of Cas's hovering over her on this very important evening unnerved her. "It might be better to meet somewhere. I'll probably want to rest for a short while after the cocktail party."

Her smile was serene, but there was an implacability to it. Cas decided not to argue. "All right, T'ang Qi. By the way, are you married?"

"Are you?" She watched him. His eyes narrowed and darkened, a muscle at the side of his mouth jumped.

"I was," he said. "I'm not now."

"I suppose in many ways I'll always be married, but I shall meet you for dinner." She held out her hand. "Perhaps you could give me the address where we'll be meeting. Then I must say goodbye. There are people I must speak with and I'm sure you're busy."

She was brushing him off! Cas hadn't been given a fast shuffle in years! Women just didn't do that to him. He wrote down the address, handed it to her, and watched as she walked away. Alone, chagrined, off balance, he ground his teeth in frustration. What the hell was he going to do with the rest of the day? He didn't want to go back to his office. Damn her! He'd only known her an hour and already she'd upset his routine.

He left the gallery and began walking up Madison Avenue. It was too warm for January. It should've been storming. Instead the sun shone, people had forgone hats and gloves, and many of them were even smiling. It was unreal for Manhattan. Had T'ang Qi done that? He was going bonkers.

He looked up and realized he'd walked to his own place not far from Central Park. Grimacing he took out his house key. His houseman, Dannler, was too well trained to look surprised when he met him in the foyer, but he did blink. "Are you ill, sir?"

"No, just taking the day off."

Dannler did look taken aback then. "And about time, sir. Can I get you anything?"

"Yes, a drink. Make it Saratoga water."

"Did you say Saratoga water, sir?" That rocked Dannler. His employer had been drinking quarts of Irish whiskey since his wife died.

"No ice," Cas said abruptly. "And lay out my evening clothes. I'm taking a lady to dinner."

Well, that was familiar. His employer had had a string of "ladies" in the past two years. Dannler hadn't approved of his employer's way of life, but what could he do?

Four

The maître d' at Benedict's eyed Mr. Griffith warily. He'd had two double whiskeys since his arrival, and he'd just signaled the waiter again. Gaston had trained in Paris; he knew how to handle any situation . . . but he didn't relish dealing with the mercurial and powerful Mr. Griffith. He'd seen him in action before when he'd had that same brooding look. Gaston quelled a delicate shudder at the memory of overturned tables, women screeching like hunting falcons, and men roaring like bulls in the arena. He couldn't believe it when old-time waiters at Benedict's, such as Andre, told him that Mr. Griffith hadn't always been so belligerent. Gaston would've bet the Eiffel Tower that Mr. Griffith had been born that way.

"Pardon me," Margo said. "I'm meeting someone. Perhaps you might tell me if my host has arrived." She glanced in the direction of the maître d's stare and answered her own question.

So, she thought. It would seem that Cas could be a problem if she read the expression on the master of the house's face correctly. Laughter rose in her again. Cas had always had an undercurrent of wildness in him, but she'd only seen it manifested in their bedroom. When they'd been in company, or even alone, he'd always been the soul of decorum . . . except that first day on the Seven Seas Lagoon. He'd shown a hint of the barbarian that day. And she'd loved him ten minutes after meeting him. Or was it five? Or at first glance?

Were they still tied by their vows? she wondered suddenly. Well, no matter what the legal state might be, she had no intention of letting her husband just slide away. She'd fight for him. And she'd begin the battle with this dinner. Up the rebels.

She was glad she'd taken a good bit of time with her toilette, even if she was late. Gaining back Cas might be like waging war.

"Forgive me, madame," Gaston said. "Your name, please." She was a rare beauty, he mused. Eastern? Mostly. So many Eastern women had that winsomeness that he'd once associated only with French women. Her style was as Gallic as her haute couture gown. French oriental. Delightful.

"T'ang Qi," she answered him.

"Ah, yes, Miss T'ang. How nice to see you. Mr. Griffith is waiting for you."

It was the answer to Gaston's prayers. This woman might be just the person to handle the unpredictable Mr. Griffith . . . if that could be done. But then, he couldn't get his hopes up. Mr. Griffith had had a woman with him when he'd smashed the crystal vase against the banquette mirror. Gaston shuddered. *Ma foi,* why did such things have to happen to a hardworking son of Marseilles?

Gesturing to the beautiful woman to follow him, he hurried across the room, trying to beat the waiter bringing another double Irish to number seven, the best table in the house.

Cas sensed her presence before he looked up, then he caught her elusive fragrance. He shot to his feet, ignoring Gaston's slightly elevated eyebrow.

"I thought you weren't coming," he blurted, then frowned. He was downright puerile with her.

He seated her on the banquette himself, preferring the anonymity that such an arrangement provided. He'd ordered the table specifically to give them a measure of privacy. He couldn't take his eyes off her. She was gorgeous. Her peach satin dress clung to her, enhancing the wonder of her skin, giving it the bloom of a Peace rose, pinky cream. The dress emphasized her eyes, too, turning them to star sapphires. Both the skin and eyes had fooled him. He'd thought earlier that her skin was more sallow, her eyes more hazel than blue. She *did* have his wife's coloring! How had he been tricked? Was she a chameleon? Or was it the whiskey? Maybe her eyes were black, the flickering candles making them seem blue. Hadn't they been green that morning? No. Blue.

He caught his breath as she allowed her matching satin shawl to drift down her back, baring her shoulders. The hint of full breasts at the top of her dress drew his gaze. His heart thudded heavily. Desire for her galloped through him.

"Forgive my tardiness," she said. "I was longer at the gallery than I wanted to be." That was true, Margo thought. But she was late for dinner because she'd lost her courage a few times, then she hadn't been able to decide on what to wear. She'd purchased some French designer dresses in London, but nothing had seemed appropriate. Finally she'd donned the first garment she'd taken from the closet. She eyed the drink in front of Cas, the glitter in his eyes. "You've been here for some time, I see." Other than an occasional glass of wine or champagne, she'd rarely seen Cas drink. Though his skin was taut, there was a hint of redness around his eyes, a floridness to his flesh that told her it was a rarity no longer.

He followed her glance to his glass and nodded. "Would you like an aperitif?" he asked, gesturing to the waiter.

"I'll have mineral water and lime, please," she said.

"I'll have the same." Cas glared at the waiter when he looked startled. "I've had enough whiskey." Why was he explaining? Irritation built in him. What was behind that serene smile of hers? He'd been damn sure that she'd stood him up. Now he had a feeling she was laughing at him. He didn't like it. "Shall we have something to start?"

She shook her head. "I should like a sorbet following my dinner, instead, I think. If not a sorbet, perhaps a *tiramisu*, if they have it. I'm very partial to that." She felt reckless, on the brink. She'd tell him tonight . . . but later. Teasing him

first titillated her more than she'd have imagined.
She could have laughed out loud at the fun of it.

"An Italian dessert? Have you lived in Europe?"
Dammit, why hadn't he read up on her? He'd
assumed she'd spent her life in China.

"I've skied in Italy." She looked away from him,
cutting off a rejoinder, smiling at the waiter when
he returned with their drinks. She noted that Cas
downed the rest of his whiskey when the waiter
placed the mineral water in front of him. He
seemed on the brink of something. Yes, there was
definitely a tension in him, a reckless gleam in
those wonderful green eyes.

"Let me order for you," he said. "Do you mind?"
Cas stared at her, feeling sensual, powerful. He
could have eaten her with a sugar spoon, one tiny
bite at a time.

The young Margo would have let him. He'd
often ordered for both of them after they were
married. The waiter was already turning deferen-
tially toward Cas. "No, thank you," she said. "I'll
order my own food. I know what I like."

Mouth agape, the waiter turned back to her,
his pad and pencil drooping loosely in his flaccid
fingers. No one ever went up against Mr. Griffith.
It wasn't good policy. The waiter glanced at the
banquette mirror to catch Griffith's expression.
He looked stunned. The waiter quickly turned
back to the lovely lady.

Cas had just taken a swallow of the mineral
water. In surprise, he swallowed more than he'd
intended. His throat muscles constricted, and he
coughed roughly, several times. Blank or slightly
irate glances came from other tables, but he

couldn't stop coughing. He was furious! Helpless. He couldn't control the coughing. Damn her. Did she say she'd order for herself? Through a haze of tears and frustration he saw her rise gracefully from her seat. Dammit! Where was she going? He couldn't move.

"I'll take care of this," Margo said gently. The alarmed waiter nodded. She brought up her arm, and in a quick downward chop, she hit Cas with the side of her hand, not too hard. It was a well-aimed blow, the power at the right pitch.

Smack! Cas pitched forward, the liquid that had blocked his throat jettisoning onto the table. Christ! he thought. He was spitting up all over the place. Painfully, he inhaled at last, his spasm spent. He lifted his head, watching her as she just as gracefully resumed her seat. There was a tiny quiver at the corner of her mouth. She *was* laughing at him! He glared at her, then at the hovering waiter. "Miss T'ang will order," he said.

"Yes, sir." The glassy-eyed waiter turned like a robot to Margo, unobtrusively signaling a lesser minion to replace the cloth and reset the table.

"I'd like to start with a Caesar salad," Margo said, "then the broiled mahimahi with brown rice." She closed the two-foot-high menu with a decided snap and, smiling, handed it to the waiter.

"I'll have the same with a baked potato," Cas said hoarsely, his raw throat working over the words. He shoved the cloth-covered cardboard at the attendant.

"Wine?" Cas asked.

"No, thank you," Margo said sweetly. When had

she ever had such fun? T'ang had told her to be open, to say what she felt, though without being blunt. Tonight bordering on blunt was delightful. It was jerking Cas's chain. Wonderful.

"No wine," Cas said abruptly, disliking Miss T'ang Qi at that moment.

"Headache?" Margo asked. She leaned forward, resting her chin on her threaded fingers. She felt confident, relaxed, in charge. That was a first. Cas had never really been off balance. Once in a while she'd sensed a restrained frustration in him, but there'd always been control. Not now. He'd become a bear . . . and she was going to try to pull his claws. She didn't resent his anger, she welcomed it. Anything was better than what they'd had before, with all the plastic responses, the sugar-coated evasions. That everlasting politeness between them that masked many true feelings. Maybe she wouldn't succeed in leveling all the barriers, but there were fewer already between them. When she told him who she was, there might be even taller walls, but she would take that chance. Truth would be in the forefront, no matter the consequences. And along the way she would let him know exactly how she felt about things, the control of her life, her presence in the universe as a woman and a person, her need to be herself. She loved him so, she needed him so. But she'd be her own person . . . and it would be the *real* Margo who got his love in return.

Cas wanted to blister her hide with words. He'd handled more than one fractious employee or client the same way. He didn't know why he smiled. "Feeling a power, are you?"

She nodded, smiling back. "And enjoying it. You're not used to that, are you?"

He sipped some of his water, made a face, and tried to swallow his annoyance. She'd gotten under his skin like a nettle, but she intrigued the hell out of him. "Maybe not. But you don't know me, either."

"Does anybody?" She held her breath when his green eyes came to bear on her like lasers.

That stung, Cas realized, shocked. How had she known what would slice right through him? How many times had he wanted to open up to Margo, yet had held back? Now he lived with that regret. More than anything in the world he wanted his wife to know him and need him, just as he needed her and wanted to know every pore of her body and soul. If only once he'd dropped his guard . . .

"I'm not sure," he said at last. "Does anyone know you?"

"I know me. That's enough."

Her serenity bowled him over. Sitting back in his chair, he swirled the mineral water in his glass, watching the bobbing lime slice. He felt analyzed, exposed, and yet they hadn't exchanged any real personal information. As he sat there the music from the other room penetrated. It was a Latin group and they were playing music for the lambada.

He glanced at her. "Shall we dance?"

The startled blink of her eyes buoyed him. It was refreshing to know something could put T'ang Qi off the mark. He placed his glass on the table and rose, going around to her side and taking hold of her arm, urging her toward him.

It was either slide across the bench toward him or be dragged, Margo thought. She could see the purpose in his eyes. Besides, it had always been fun dancing with Cas. Like many tall men, he was graceful and rhythmic. And they'd danced the lambada the first night they'd met. It was so sexy. The thought of dancing it with him again made her hot all over. Still, there was that alien glitter in his eyes that she'd seen when he'd held the purse snatcher. Her heart thudded against her ribs. What did he have in mind?

As they threaded their way through the tables, Margo noticed a couple of faces that looked familiar. Some people gazed at her, most looked at the man behind her. She saw avidity on more than one set of female features. Well, they'd have to fight her for him. She was back and she wanted her husband.

She stopped on the threshold of the other room, her eyes widening. The people doing the lambada were really into it.

Cas grinned at her. As she turned her head, he could tell she was thinking of changing her mind. Grasping her firmly around the waist, he led her to the floor, then swept her into his arms, plastering her to his chest. The first time his leg slid between hers he heard her gasp. He could feel her indecision. She was uncertain. But so was he. When he felt the wonderful junction of her body on his leg, blood thundered through him. His body hardened in response. Keeping her close to him, his eyes barely open, he bent and swayed to the rapid beat.

At first Margo was stunned at how desire flooded her. She felt conquered, consumed, over-taken by the heat his nearness engendered. They might go up in smoke! Then his heat permeated her, and her body betrayed her. It trembled with the familiar want that only Cas could cause. She turned pliant, her body following his as they swayed, dipped, bent, and circled around the floor. She forgot everything in the pulsing, thrust-ing steps, the music pushing, taking, forcing the dancing that was so sexually appealing. She barely heard the smattering of applause, though a part of her was aware that others were watching them. She couldn't have pulled back from him without tearing herself apart. Her face was lifted to his, her eyes closed. The throbbing beat imi-tated the rush of blood through her.

"You're very good at this, Qi," he whispered.

She stiffened. She hadn't given him permission to use her first name, but he'd done it. Among the people with whom she'd lived, it was important to be impersonal until one knew another well. Had he guessed that she wouldn't mind? Did he know? Suspect? "I like the dance." She looked up into his eyes and smiled.

He missed a step and gave her back her con-fidence.

It seemed eons before the dance finished. Margo couldn't hear the applause and compliments over the roaring in her ears.

"That was wonderful, Qi," Cas whispered sen-sually.

Smile in place, she preceded him from the dance floor, out of breath, warm, wanting, needful. When the casual hand at her waist squeezed, she stiffened again, but didn't stop. The table was like a haven to her. She needed to get there before her rubbery knees gave way.

When she sat down, Cas was at her side on the banquette, not opposite her as he had been. She glanced at him warily, then tried to pull back. She couldn't move and his mouth was a centimeter from hers.

"What did you think of the dance?" he asked.

"Very expressive." It had been downright graphic. They'd all but made love on the floor. Exciting. Demanding. Wonderful.

"Had you ever done it before?" In spite of her stoical facade he knew she'd been shocked. But she'd been good at the dance. "I like it," he added. "I've danced it many times."

"All over town, no doubt," she said tartly, then could have bitten her tongue. His low laugh made her shiver. He sounded positively Svengalian.

"Sometimes. But I promise to—"

"No need to promise anything you might not be able to keep," she said hurriedly. Damn. She wanted to know what he'd been going to say. Why was she such a coward? "Ah, here's our first course."

"Saved by the bell," Cas murmured in her ear, letting his breath feather the sensitive skin there. When she frowned, he pulled back, smiling at her. Then he turned to watch the waiter quickly mix their salads. "That looks good, doesn't it?"

"Yes." Her appetite was fading fast, and so was

her confidence. Damn him. That dance had almost put him in the driver's seat. She'd been shaken to her shoes, but she'd loved it. She was so hot for him. She needed him. She took deep breaths and said her mantra to herself.

"What are you saying?" Cas hadn't caught the sound, but he'd seen the infinitesimal movement of her lips.

"My mantra," she said reluctantly. T'ang had explained that not all followers of the serene path employed such a method to call on peace. T'ang didn't use a mantra. She found it bolstering. And she needed it desperately at the moment. "It's soothing," she added, "more of a key to tap into my inner strength than a prayer."

"It's to stiffen your spine or buck you up, isn't it?" Cas said. "Do you need that with me, Qi?" It delighted him to think she had to call on a buffer when she was with him. Why should he be the only one off balance?

"Yes," she admitted hesitantly, "but it's more. It's to remind a person of her place in the universe, to understand that the flow continues with or without her, to give strength, and humility."

The mantra had calmed her. Cas disturbed her more than she'd thought possible. The dance had brought back all the sensuality that had been so much a part of their lives in the past. If they were to have a future, real dialogue and honesty were a must.

She ached to really know Cas, to peel back the layers of secrets between them. With all she'd learned from her mentor and what she'd read in the works of the old masters, she knew that she would never waste time being evasive again. Truth and a direct way of speaking were woven into her now. She was going to connect with Cas as soon as possible. If he rejected her, it wouldn't be because she'd held back. Those days were gone forever. She wanted it all, the words, the gestures, the glances, and most of all, the loving. When they were dancing, that had been shown to her graphically. His touch had been magic, torrid, tender. It was as though they'd been in bed. They'd been alive in every sense of the word . . . dancing. And their bodies had spoken loud and clear.

"I want to speak to you with all of me," she murmured.

"What?" Cas couldn't believe what she'd just said. "Say that again."

"There's no need. You'll understand everything."

"At this moment I understand nothing," he muttered, but he didn't push. He was content to let her words lie suspended over them.

They ate their food almost in rhythm, the forks moving from plate to mouth, slowly, carefully, as though if they didn't do it to some hidden cadence, they couldn't. They pondered, glanced at each other for long moments, smiled tentatively. There was much to know. It was companionable, but wary. It was the threshold of a new life, or the closing of a door.

Cas had ambivalent feelings. He tamped them down, not believing what he felt. Earlier, she'd responded to another cliché remark of his, as though she used American colloquialisms comfortably. Had she lived here at another time? And that cryptic remark she'd made. What did she mean? And there was the other sensation he didn't like examining, but it ballooned in his mind. When he'd been dancing with Qi, it had been as though he'd held Margo in his arms. Yet Qi was nothing like Margo. . . . Well, maybe the hair color was the same, but the style was different. The height was the same, but the structures were different. Margo had been more voluptuous, yet Qi, though slimmer, was curvy too. Margo had had a very sexy body, but so did Qi.

Cas was twisted inside. He was very attracted to the oriental-occidental beauty, but his dead wife kept getting in the way. That had happened at other times, yet he'd always been able to put Margo out of his mind for a short while when he was with another woman. Not this time. It was like an itch he couldn't scratch.

The lambada wasn't played again, but they danced to both fast and slow numbers after dining.

"You're a very good dancer," he said at one point. "Did you dance often in China?"

"No." Cas was filled with questions, Margo thought. That amused her. He could be patient for a short time longer. And she'd be on tenterhooks for a little longer, wondering what his reaction would be when she told him who she was. She didn't resist when he took her hand as they returned to the table.

"Then did you learn to dance in other countries?" he asked.

"Yes." She ate the last of her dessert and rose,

disconcerting him. She really enjoyed that. "We're ready to leave, aren't we?"

Cas stared up at her, taken aback. Then he stood. "Yes. I guess we are." He dashed his name across the back of the bill and reached for her stole. But she donned it before he could touch it. She was damned elusive . . . in every way. She didn't go into detail about her life, she put him off in many ways.

"Has a man been cruel to you, Qi?" he asked as he helped her with her coat. He felt her stiffen as though the question had surprised her. When she would have pushed open the outside door, he held it closed. "Well? Was a man cruel to you?"

Margo gazed up at those piercing eyes, inhaling a shuddering breath. "Not intentionally."

"What does that mean?"

"Just what I said." She smiled. "Shall we go?"

"Yes." Damn her! "Do you want to wait here? The valet isn't around, but I know where the car is."

She shook her head. "I could use a breath of fresh air." She put her hand through his arm, smiling when he looked startled.

They both inhaled deeply of the crisp night air. A cold white moon shone like a beacon above.

He cast around in his mind for some questions to ask her. Not that he hoped for a straight answer. She was a master at obliqueness. "Do you prefer sculpting to painting?"

"It depends on the subject I'm considering. Some things lend themselves more to painting than sculpting, and vice versa." She smiled, feeling his frustration. "Anything else you'd like to know?"

"Yes. Everything." He couldn't stem a smile when she laughed out loud.

"Soon, you'll know it all," she said enigmatically, squeezing his arm.

"I wish I knew what you mean by that." He paused and turned her to face him. "You must know I'm interested in you."

"You're a fast worker, as Americans say." She liked to watch the play of lights from the street and cars scroll across his tough features.

He took hold of her face, his large hands cupping her cheeks. "And you're a fisherwoman, with me hooked through the jaw and dangling from your line."

"Ooo, sounds painful." She laughed. It was wonderful to have him touch her. She wanted him so much. He was happiness to her.

"Tell me about t'ai chi. I know it's a martial art. How is it that you mastered it?" Cas noted how the streetlights made her skin glow. She was incredibly beautiful.

"I'm not a master, but a pupil. *Qi cong* is a medical treatment that was used on me. Since t'ai chi is related to it, it seemed a natural thing to learn. With t'ai chi one can maim and kill. I was taught to use it for defense only."

Cas loved the sound of her voice, its musical cadence. Margo had lilting tones. Damn. He wasn't going to dwell on her.

"Tell me where you studied art. Paris?"

"I never studied formally, though I did dabble in painting and sculpting in college."

Again her answer was quick and to the point, but he felt put off, as though she'd hedged with him, not told him the whole truth. That made him more anxious to dig away until he got it.

"Your English is perfect and unaccented, and your white skin says you're not totally oriental." They'd reached his car. He unlocked and opened the passenger door, then faced her again.

"Almost, though," she said cryptically.

He shut her door with a snap, then walked around the back of the car. "I'm going to find out why you're toying with me, lady," he muttered. Despite his frustration, he couldn't help but smile. She was damned intriguing. When he got behind the wheel, he didn't start the car right away. Instead he turned and looked at her, shaking his head.

"What is it?" she asked, her voice unsteady. She melted at the hot urgency of his gaze.

"I know you and I don't know you."

"It seems that way, but it'll change."

"You bet it will. I'm going to know you." Cas hit the wheel with the flat of his hand, then started the car and pulled smoothly into Manhattan traffic that even at this time of night was heavy.

Margo chuckled. His lower lip stuck out like a determined little boy's. Cas was adorable. She bloomed like a June rose at his words. Did he want to keep her? She wanted to keep him, caress him, love him, forever.

His head swiveled her way. "Why are you laughing?"

"You're cute when you're angry," she said huskily.

"Will you come to my place for a drink?" He couldn't say good night to her just yet.

Since she'd been about to suggest that very thing, she smiled. "Of course."

"Of course?" He glanced at her, then back to the traffic when horns blared at him. What in hell was going on? It couldn't be the whiskey. But he felt bleary. He blinked at the traffic ahead. Was the car in front of them weaving?

"There's somebody who should be off the road. Drunk, I'll bet." Margo pointed at the vehicle directly in front of them. She heard Cas's sudden exhalation. "What was that for?"

"Starting to question my perceptions, I guess." He glanced at her. "You did say you'd have a nightcap with me?"

She nodded, settling back with a sigh.

Cas was puzzled. She looked so . . . serene, as though it had been her idea to go to his place. She confused him. At times he seemed to know her, other times she was a stranger.

He accelerated, threading through traffic like a race driver. Margo winced. "Ah, I'd like to get there alive."

The car slowed, but not appreciably. "I can handle a car. I've done some racing."

"Oh? When?" The images of the many accidents she'd seen involving racing, particularly at the Memorial Day Classic, catapulted through her mind. That Cas could've been in something like that was appalling. She gulped air at the pain such a vision produced.

"Last year. Just local racing, nothing big-time.

I did manage to win more than I lost." He shot her a quick grin. "I'm bragging."

"That's something to brag about," she said lightly, her heart thudding against her breastbone as she imagined him among a thunderous cacophony of speeding machines. Her being somersaulted with terror. "Why?" she whispered.

"Huh? Oh, I guess because it's there." And last year he'd wanted to die or be permanently unconscious, or not think for twenty years. "My wife's uncle sponsored me. I guess he needed the diversion too."

"Diversion? Surely risking your life is more than that." Her heart squeezed inside her. Cas had suffered. And poor Uncle Ivor. He must have been so hurt. She'd have to speak to him as soon as possible. Yet she'd have to be careful too. She didn't want to shock him. Oh, that was silly. No matter how she approached him, he'd be stunned.

"What are you thinking, Qi?"

"I'm thinking you had pain, as did those around you."

She turned on the seat and faced him fully. She watched his features tighten as emotions flooded him. She realized that she was turning the key, opening a rusty door he'd have preferred left shut. She could almost hear the protesting squeaking of the dark corners of his mind. But the only soothing oil would be their communication, the total eradication of the black side that lack of openness had brought to their relationship. No more enabling silences that had torn at the fabric of their marriage. Releasing the frozen lock on their feelings would be agonizing. But if they didn't do it, sweep it all out into the light, they'd always be on half power, no matter if they got back together or not.

Five

Déjà vu almost swamped her as they rode up in the elevator from the garage to the apartment. Her home! Though she hadn't spent much time in it, she'd always perceived it that way. When the elevator doors opened right into the cream-colored foyer that she'd decorated—some before they married, the rest with overseas phone calls—her knees almost buckled. The French cloth wallpaper in swirls of cream, coral, and pewter was richly understated, the colors imitating the pewter chandelier with its cranberry glass base. She and Cas had prowled the English countryside on one of their side trips there and had found the chandelier at a manor house auction. It had cost the earth, but Cas had quickly outbid all others and presented it to her. Her throat was so constricted she couldn't swallow for a moment. She hadn't expected the rush of weakness, the welling tears. It took all her effort not to sink to the floor and sob her heart out. Home.

"Nice," she said hoarsely.

"Thank you." Qi had hesitated before leaving the elevator, Cas noticed. Had she changed her mind? There was so much he didn't know about her. He'd almost said that Margo had decorated the two-story foyer, that she'd added all the little touches that made it beautiful and homey. Instead, he bit his lip and smiled at his guest. He wasn't going to mention his wife again. Margo had intruded enough for one night.

He took Qi's coat and gazed at her. "I know I'm repeating myself, but you do look wonderful in that peach satin. You glow." When she turned and smiled, her eyes drooping sensuously, he almost dropped her coat. That look! Margo used to do that. Margo again! Dammit. Go away.

"Headache?" she asked huskily. "You frowned."

"No, I was just wondering how you'd react if I picked you up, raced up the stairs, laid you on my bed, then made passionate love to you."

Damn! he thought. That had just burst forth from the back of his brain. What in hell was the matter with him? He stared at her, willing her to forgive him. He'd just committed the social gaffe of the century with a woman he wanted to treasure. If she went screaming into the night, he couldn't blame her. Maybe he needed therapy.

He was doing everything wrong. He hadn't really planned to bring her to his home. He had another apartment two blocks away where he'd taken other women. Something had impelled him to bring her here. He hoped Margo wouldn't come out of the woodwork. She'd been everywhere else that evening. Now he wanted privacy.

"Qi, I—"

"Why don't you try it and see?" Margo asked. The idea of being carried up to his bedroom and making love after those long months without him was enough to make her want to drag him bodily up there herself. Lord! She was actually salivating. She ached to kiss him, embrace him with her whole self, love that wonderful male body until morning.

"Try what?" he asked in obvious disbelief.

"You suggested it. How could you have forgotten so soon?"

"I don't know. Ah . . . maybe you'd better spell it out for me this time," he said weakly. What an inane remark! he berated himself. All his sophistication had melted into clumsiness. Since he'd met the woman, he'd been in an advanced stage of cerebral deterioration. It had to stop.

"All right," she said. "Why don't we have a drink and discuss it. You could loosen your tie . . . and other things." She scored one fingernail down his chest, smiling into his eyes. Then she turned and walked away from him.

He was dying in his own front hall! Cas thought. He couldn't get a breath, couldn't swallow, couldn't move. He couldn't believe his ears either. Had she just invited him to undress? No. Don't be stupid. As she walked toward the living room— seeming to know exactly where it was—he could only watch, admiring her cool confidence. In some ways she was so sure of herself, yet in others she was surprisingly naive. He loved the amalgam. Thank goodness she hadn't jumped back into the elevator. She must not have believed he was serious about taking her up to bed. Her answer had been provocative and flirtatious . . . but innocent too. He'd have to be careful with her. He could frighten her.

He followed her into the spacious room, its cream-colored furnishings accented with touches of Wedgwood green and blue. A mammoth oval Kirman rug, in creams, blues, greens, and corals, dominated the area. "What can I get you?" he asked huskily.

"Champagne, I think, though not too much. I wouldn't want anything to dull my senses . . . not now." Margo turned around and looked into Cas's wonderful emerald eyes. They had a sensual glint that sent her head spinning. "I like this room. It suits you. And I like you, Lancaster Griffith."

Cas stopped dead, his mouth dropping open at her sultry tone, the hot look in her eyes. His hands shook, and he had to fight for control. He couldn't misunderstand that look. Could he? For a moment he felt caught by the warmth in her eyes. Margo again. Go away! "I'll have champagne too," he managed to say at last.

She followed him to the bar in the corner, watching as he pulled a bottle from the small refrigerator. When he poured the bubbly wine, she reached under his arm for a glass, her body pressed to his back. "Looks good."

"Dom . . . Dom . . . it is." He was stuttering like a schoolboy! he thought. He hadn't even been able to say Dom Pérignon!

Pressed tighter to him now, from shoulder to knee, Margo brought the glass back beneath his arm and sipped. She could feel the tension in his body. He hadn't moved. "Have some." She reached around him to offer her glass, her breasts pressed to his arm as she shifted to one side.

He saw the pale, pale smudge of her lipstick on the glass. He drank thirstily, his tongue wiping at the smudge. "Good."

"Isn't it." She slipped her arms around his waist and pressed her face to his back, still holding the glass. "'But there are other, tastier things."

Turning carefully in her hold, he removed the glass from her hand and placed it on the bar, then let his arms fall gently around her. "True. I know I'd like to taste you." Her lazy smile melted him, then set him on fire. It was as though desire had taken on a new luster, a higher intensity, a raw but smooth thrust.

"Shall I pour champagne on myself, or would you like me plain?" she inquired huskily.

"Either way." He bent and kissed the corner of her mouth. "You didn't get much wine on your lips." Without releasing her, he reached for the glass again.

"Maybe my appetite for first-class wine has changed . . . to something else." She wanted him so much and was getting impatient with his reticence. She wanted to make love with him in every room in the apartment, in every way possible. Couldn't he feel the want throbbing through her? What did she have to do? Hit him with a club and drag him up there by the hair?

Cas sipped more champagne, trying to control the desire pulsing through his body. He had to do something! Sexual need was building like lava behind a thin crust of mountain. Maybe he could distract himself. Name the winning World Series pitchers back to 1940 or something. Damn, he wanted her. She was so damned sexy . . . so fragile.

Margo leaned back and looked up at him. She was seducing her own husband. What fun. "I've had enough to drink. But maybe we could carry it with us when you show me the upstairs." His eyes widened, the sexual glitter deepening, and her pulses raced. Her Cas was a sexy animal.

"We could do that." Keeping her close to his side, he lifted her glass and the bottle in one hand. "Shall we go?"

"At last," she murmured. She reached up and pulled his head down to hers, standing on tiptoe to kiss him. Her tongue traced his lips before entering his mouth and touching his. The slight rattle of the glass against the champagne bottle satisfied her. She was breaking through her husband's barriers. She pulled back a fraction, her heart hammering. "I wanted to see if I could taste the champagne on you."

"And?" His voice was barely audible.

"Just a hint of bubbly," she said, chuckling. Her eyes closed, her body swaying even closer to him.

"Qi!' he said brokenly, pulling her against him. As his mouth descended, he was aware over the roaring in his ears that she'd sighed with satisfaction. She wasn't frightened of him! When she opened her mouth under his, he thought his heart would burst. Bending down, he tightened his grip on her waist, lifting her up his body,

slanting his mouth across hers, his tongue questing. Without lifting his mouth, he moved slowly
across the room, memory guiding him, since all
his focus was on Qi. At the stairs he pulled back
slightly and smiled at her, loving her.

She slipped her arms around his neck. "Don't
break the glass," she whispered against his
mouth.

"Never," he whispered back. Her breath feathered over his face like a caress. He loved it. His
one foot kicked the bottom step and he started to
climb.

"Even if you do," she said, "we could always
drink from the bottle." Her mouth slid across his
cheek to his neck, then she nipped at his earlobe.
She was suspended in his one arm, her feet
swinging free. She didn't even look when her
shoes dropped off, one by one. "Umm, you have
a nice flavor."

"No more, please," Cas said hoarsely. She was
so tiny, so light. "Darling, you're like a feather."

He took the stairs two at a time, thinking that
she was magic. She had fire, sweetness, beauty,
and she was with him in his home, and he was
going to love her, keep her if she let him.

"This will be a wonderful night, darling. I promise," he said as he carried her into his bedroom.

Heady with triumph, Margo scarcely heard him.
She'd waited so long, wanted him more each
minute since she'd found him again at the gallery. Loving Cas was part of her being, threaded
through her blood, her entire system. But it
hadn't been until she'd seen him again that she'd
realized the intensity of her love. Time away from

him had watered down the memory of their great passion. She looked around the bedroom that had been theirs for such a short time. The cream, blue, and turquoise color scheme was the same. The huge round bed still dominated the room. When he set her down on it, she smiled up at him. "It's comfy." She opened her arms.

"Yes." Cas groaned at the invitation in her eyes, kneeling down in front of her. "You're wonderful. You've made me come alive."

"I hope so," she said, smiling, tracing one finger down his cheek. "I want you to make me come alive as well." Until that moment she hadn't admitted to herself that a part of her had been in limbo for two years, that all the time she'd worked her way back to good health, she'd been journeying home to him. She pushed back on the bed, straightening out her legs, quite aware that her skirt had ridden up to her thighs. "Shall I undress?" she asked. "Or would you like to do it for me?" She pulled the shawl from her shoulders and tossed it at a side chair. It missed and hit the floor. Too bad. When she would have unzipped her dress, he stopped her.

"I'll do it." With his hands on her hips, he pulled her toward him. Her slip and dress rode higher, exposing her lacy garter belt, the bare tops of her thighs, with flesh silkier than her hose. The top of her strapless dress drooped lower, pulling his gaze. "You're beautiful," he whispered.

"Thank you." So was he and she desired him.

She urged his head down to her thigh. His fingers tightened on her in delight as his tongue laved the exposed flesh. Blood pounded through him. With his hands under arms he pulled her to her feet.

"I'd better undress you quickly," he said, "or we'll be loving fully clothed."

She nodded, leaning against his chest, giving herself completely to him. "You don't have to be too careful with my things," she said. "I have other clothing."

"Don't spoil my fun. This is all the joys of Christmas unwrapping I've ever done and more."

She smiled, then began to undress him. When her fingers fought with a button on his trousers, she cursed.

Cas laughed shakily. "You're no more eager than I, darling."

"I wish I wasn't hurrying so," she said plaintively. "But I can't help it."

"Tell me about it." He pressed his mouth to her neck. "I want you, Qi."

"And I want you." She moved her head so that their lips met in a long, drenching, soul-twisting kiss of want and need, of shared passion, all earthly delights.

Then Cas was gentle no longer. His mouth was hot, hungry, and wild.

Margo didn't know how she got to her feet, how the rest of her clothes were dispatched so rapidly, or how she got back onto the bed and under the covers. She didn't care. At long last she was where she wanted to be.

They were breast to breast, lying on their sides, facing each other, mouths fused. Hands touched everywhere. Hearts thundered together, as though they were one. It was a blinding assault on the senses, and they sought the wondrous, powerful crescendo eagerly.

Passion worked its magic, and Margo felt undone, spiritually as well as physically, all the threads she'd woven into her new self unraveled. Wonderfully vulnerable, she clung to the man who'd once initiated her into sweet, sensual love. At last he was with her again, and so was the awesome joy. But even as she spiraled into delight, a part of her knew that this very night she could reach the apex of sensuousness, and the deepest despair. She shut out the warning voices and clung to her husband.

When Cas heard the whimpering sounds she made, his libido built to volcanic heat. His tongue slid in and out of her mouth in sensual cadence, each thrust taking more, giving more. He was on a roaring train, an out-of-control roller coaster. His mouth moved to the side of her neck, his tongue flicking over her ear, darting in and out again, edging the gentle curve.

He had never thought to feel such heat again. Never had the word *love* entered his vocabulary with anyone other than Margo. Yet that love, the tenderness, the desire to give all of himself was sweeping through him, and only Margo had been able to cause that in him. He didn't want to think of his dead wife, but she was more alive to him each second that he was falling more deeply in love with Qi.

"What is it?" Margo asked as he stiffened. "Did I scratch you?"

"No, darling, you didn't scratch me, but you

can if you like," Cas told her hoarsely. Her throaty laugh added more flame to his passion. He was falling in love with T'ang Qi! Groaning, he tightened his grip on her. He wanted her. He wanted to love her. He desired her passion, her body, and her spirit, and even more he wanted to give her all of his. He wanted her body to engulf him for eternity.

His mouth moved over hers possessively as he delighted in the sweet strength of her arms holding him. This time he would speak of his love, not just show it. She'd hear the words from him, even if she told him to go to hell. He drove the tortured memories of his wife from his mind, those moments when he'd wanted to tell her how much he loved her, yet had held back. Silently, he vowed that his new love would know all his thoughts about her.

Heat blasted through Margo when the rough-smooth hair on his chest massaged her breasts, tickling, titillating, hardening her nipples. She wanted more and wriggled closer, clutching him to her. It was like that other life with Cas. No. It was better, because once there'd been barriers between them. Tonight Cas would know all her feelings and emotions, how tied she was to him and had always been.

"You're so sweet, love," he murmured. "When you growl deep in your throat like that, I feel like I'm going to explode." He ran his tongue down her cheek.

"I know, I know. I feel the same. It's wonderful." She was out of breath, almost out of control, and so happy. She cupped his face, letting her tongue trail around the outside of his mouth. He was so still, but she could feel his heart pounding. She reveled in arousing him as he'd aroused her. She opened her mouth against his in pure carnal need, and he responded with such wildness, she moaned and writhed in desire.

"No one else has ever loved me like this," she told him truthfully.

"Your words are music to my soul." His hands stroked her up and down, up and down, probing, testing every pore. Her skin was unadulterated joy to him. It heated, fired, and melted him.

His growled words excited her to fever pitch. Her body responded by bucking gently against his arousal, and the warm, tingling sensation in her middle made her gasp. The world was a kaleidoscope of pink and purple lights that burst behind her eyes. Her lids were heavy, but her body felt light as helium. She loved the contrast and cuddled closer to the man who was giving her such joy. "Oh, I want you."

"Darling!" Cas pulled back from her a fraction, studying her, loving her face, her expressions. He blinked at a sudden jolt of déjà vu, then shook it off. For a moment it was as though he'd always known her. Her eyes were Margo's! No, dammit. No.

Her fingers caressed his mouth and chin. "What is it?" she asked. "You had the most surprised look on your face."

"I've been having strange reactions since I met you." He grinned ruefully when she laughed. "I have."

The Publisher of Loveswept® Romances invites you to:

CLAIM A FREE EXCLUSIVE ROMANCE

Lift Here

...PLUS SIX ROMANCES RISK FREE

6 ROMANCES FREE

NO OBLIGATION TO BUY!

THE FREE GIFT IS YOURS TO KEEP

Detach and affix this stamp to the postage-paid reply card and mail at once!

SEE DETAILS INSIDE ▶

LET YOURSELF BE LOVESWEPT BY... SIX BRAND NEW LOVESWEPT ROMANCES!

Because Loveswept romances sell themselves ...we want to send you six (Yes, six!) exciting new novels to enjoy for 15 days — risk free! — without obligation to buy.

Discover how these compelling stories of contemporary romances tug at your heart strings and keep you turning the pages. Meet true-to-life characters you'll fall in love with as their romances blossom. Experience their challenges and triumphs — their laughter, tears and passion.

Let yourself be Loveswept! Join our **at-home reader service!** Each month we'll send you six new Loveswept novels **before they appear in the bookstores.** Take up to **15 days to preview** current selections **risk-free! Keep only those shipments you want.** Each book is yours for only $2.09 plus postage & handling, and sales tax where applicable — **a savings of 41¢ per book** off the cover price.

NO OBLIGATION TO BUY — WITH THIS RISK-FREE OFFER!

YOU GET SIX ROMANCES RISK FREE...
Plus AN EXCLUSIVE TITLE FREE!

Loveswept Romances

AFFIX
RISK FREE
BOOKS
STAMP
HERE.

Kay Hooper's
Larger Than Life

This FREE gift
is yours to keep.

MY "NO RISK" GUARANTEE

There's no obligation to buy and the free gift is mine to keep. I may preview each subsequent shipment for 15 days. If I don't want it, I simply return the books within 15 days and owe nothing. If I keep them, I will pay just $2.09 per book. I save $2.50 off the retail price for the 6 books (plus postage and handling, and sales tax where applicable).

YES! Please send my six Loveswept novels
RISK FREE along with my **FREE GIFT**
described inside the heart!   **BR8**   10124

NAME_____

ADDRESS_____APT_____

CITY_____

STATE_____ZIP_____

· DETACH AND MAIL CARD TODAY ·

FREE BOOK OFFER!

**PREVIEW SIX BRAND NEW
LOVESWEPT ROMANCES RISK FREE
...PLUS A FREE EXCLUSIVE ROMANCE**

**NO PURCHASE REQUIRED
THE FREE GIFT IS YOURS TO KEEP**

BUSINESS REPLY MAIL

FIRST-CLASS MAIL   PERMIT NO. 2456   HICKSVILLE, NY

POSTAGE WILL BE PAID BY ADDRESSEE

Loveswept

Bantam Books
P.O. Box 985
Hicksville, NY 11802-9827

NO POSTAGE
NECESSARY
IF MAILED
IN THE
UNITED STATES

"Oh, I believe you. I've had a few . . . alien but familiar sensations myself."

"That's it exactly. I've felt like I've known you forever. Yet, we've just met. Maybe we were together in another life," he said softly.

"Oh, I'm sure of it," she whispered.

His body trembled, and he kissed her long and passionately. Then he gazed at her for long seconds, the warm, pliant length of her stretched out beside him. "And I want you, beautiful lady," he said, small kisses emphasizing each word. In questing gentleness he trailed his mouth down her body. When he reached her wonderful breasts, he pressed his face between them, then let his mouth slide to one nipple. Sucking tenderly, he felt as though he'd just died. He was whirled into the mystique that had claimed him since their first meeting, and he forgot all else. His mouth slid lower until it could whorl over her middle, his tongue darting in and out of her navel.

Gripping the sheets to keep from floating to the ceiling, Margo gasped as the hot emotion that had always been between her and Cas claimed her again. It was better, bigger. How could that be? It'd been so perfect before . . . yet it was better. She wanted to be suspended in time, not face the hours ahead when she would tell her husband who she was. Those revelations could kill her. She clutched him to her.

Cas looked up at her and caught her sudden worried look. Then he thought he was mistaken when she gazed at him dreamy eyed, a sensuous smile slipping on and off her face. "Ah, love, you have a rare beauty." He didn't realize he'd spoken aloud until her smile widened, and she touched the edge of his mouth with one finger.

"Thank you, Lancaster." She savored his name, running the syllables off her tongue.

"Thank you." The hand that had played with the opening at the junction of her body, had made those wonderful soft lips flower and grow wet, moved away. He slid lower and let his mouth take its place. The taste of her almost undid him, and for a moment it took all of his concentration not to explode. The soft triangle of black hair tickled his face as he pressed into her. Her soft, gasping cries had his libido thundering in answer. When her body began a slow writhing, he stilled it with his hands and pushed into her, high and sweet.

"Cas!" Margo couldn't get her breath. She whirled into the splendor that had her quaking, as though every bone in her body would fragment. Ecstasy was a welcome white fire that flared higher until it consumed her. The flood of life flowed through her and she called out her husband's name again and again.

When he felt her release, Cas quickly moved up her body, thrusting into her, taking her with a force he couldn't control, his movements matching hers as she took all of him. They rode the crest for endless moments, savoring the joy. Then they crashed together in simultaneous release, their bodies embracing, shaking, as the storm rose to an unbelievable intensity and burst over them.

"Margo! Darling! I love you!"

"Cas, I love you!"

They lay together, spent, breathing heavily, bodies spasming in joyous relief as the quaking subsided.

Margo reveled in the last vibrations of passion, not opening her eyes lest she break the spell.

He couldn't have! Cas thought in shock. He couldn't have called out his wife's name. Not then, at the climax! Was it his black imagination saying he did it? Surely he couldn't have been such a fool. He loved Qi. Grief shook him. How could he ask her to accept a man who couldn't break the ties with his dead wife?

When Cas would've pulled back from her, Margo held him. She needed the warmth a little longer. The time had come for honesty, and she felt a feathering of trepidation. They'd just made wildly wonderful love, and she needed to savor the moment, not begin the conversation that could break her marriage, that could sunder a brand-new connection in an old relationship.

"Don't move yet," she said softly. "I have something to tell you."

Cas nodded against her neck. He didn't want to face her. He didn't want to tell her that what they had was too precious to share with a third party, but Margo was still in his life. If he couldn't eradicate her at the height of passion with a woman he'd grown to love, then it wasn't time to begin a relationship. It could ultimately be destroyed by memories of his first wife. He lifted his head and gazed at her. She even looked like Margo at that moment, with her hair tousled all about her face, her lip gloss eaten off by him, her body curved indolently on his bed. God. He wanted her still. "Qi. I'm sorry."

"Don't be. I loved it."

"I loved it too. But I called out my wife's name and—"

"I heard." It was getting closer. Her mouth went dry. Her hands trembled.

"I know you're not as unaffected as you seem. I felt you tremble." He embraced her, feeling like crying. "I don't want to give you up. I love you. But our lives would be terrible if every time we made love, I called out my wife's name. It wouldn't be fair to you." He lifted his head. "You even look like her at this minute."

She touched his face, her heart wrenching at its tortured expression. "I should," she said.

"I know that you're trying to be kind, love, but it's no good. I have to resolve a lot of feelings about my wife before I can be with you. And I don't know how long it will take. It isn't fair to ask you to wait around until I get rid of my ghosts." He shook his head. "I'm so sorry, Qi. Right now I can't handle the memories. I want to be with you. But it was as though I was making love to my wife when I was holding you."

She reached up and took hold of his face. "You were."

He frowned in puzzlement. "What do you mean?"

"I'm your wife, Margo, and I'm Qi."

Cas reared back from her as though she'd struck at him. "That's not funny," he said tautly. "I'm not into fantasies that would make a ghost part of a ménage à trois."

"I'm not being funny, Lancaster McCross Griffith." But all at once a weird humor assailed her. Laughter burst out of her as Cas's horror grew. "You have to admit that there's a touch of the bizarre here. The spirit of your wife in a ménage à trois? Wow. I never recall you being so innovative, Cas. When did this come on? I thought I was the one steeped in oriental mystique."

He leaped off the bed when she reached out to him, his body quivering. "What the hell is the matter with you? You need a doctor."

She sat up in bed, pulling the sheet to her chin and staring into his eyes. "I'm your wife, Margo. Mary Gottfriede Tyssen Griffith to be completely accurate."

He backed up, his naked body covered with goose bumps and cold sweat. "You're lying," he said hoarsely.

"I'm not. The plane crashed in the Himalayas, not far from Lhasa. I should've died. The others did. Somehow I got out of the plane and wandered through the snow. I must've been delirious. I was found by lamas who took me to their lamasery. I nearly died there. I was in a coma for some time, then in and out of consciousness. They had no drugs to treat me, only their ancient methods of healing. One of them is called *qi cong*. I took my first name from that treatment. My other name belongs to my mentor, T'ang." She paused, licking her lips, which had gone desert dry. "Say something."

Cas shook his head. He was paralyzed, horrified yet also feeling an alien elation, incredulity, shock. Blood seemed to fill his head, and he wondered if he was having a stroke. Anger began as a tiny hot stream. If she was Margo—and he couldn't accept that—why had she stayed away from him? Hell, she'd almost killed him.

"Believe me, it's true," she said. "I am Margo."

He shook his head again, backing away even more, his thoughts chaotic, unconnected. "My wife was not part Chinese. You can't be Margo." Anger had become a river, building, building.

"I am your wife. And I'm not Chinese, not Tibetan. It's my dark hair, but I'm Caucasian . . . outwardly. Sometimes now I think like an Oriental." She saw how he wavered, how the hot blood rose in his neck. Incredulity was fading to wariness, confusion melting slowly to puzzlement. He exhaled heavily.

"Where have you been?" The words stuck in his tight throat. He felt cheated. Overjoyed. Suspicious. Anger was becoming a cascade. He was blinded by the flood of emotion, both positive and negative.

"In the lamasery," she answered. "As I said, I was in and out of consciousness for many weeks. Even when I regained full awareness, I was often too weak to talk. At first I was too sick to do much more than to listen to my mentor read. He read to me in Chinese, then laboriously translated it into English. He was my only link to life."

"Why didn't you contact me? Contact Ivor?" Did he believe her? As he looked at her, she became more and more like Margo. The oriental hints seemed to be fading. How had he missed it? How could he not have known it was she? Oh, the features had been altered— "Your face has changed," he blurted.

She nodded, a little fearfully. "I had to have cosmetic surgery to remove scars. I was badly burned and cut in the crash. They told me it could've happened when I struggled out of the plane." She touched her cheek. "I had operations, treatments. They changed my face." Did he hate it?

"Yes." She was scarred, he thought. And she'd been hurt, alone. Wasn't she T'ang Qi? But there was an essence of Margo to her. It was not believable . . . but he'd started to accept. They'd made love! Wildly. Beautifully. Had his subconscious known her? Was that why Margo's image came to mind when he'd caressed Qi? "Tell me what happened."

"When I began to recover, I realized I'd probably been considered dead for many months." She looked away from him for a moment, frowning. "I can't describe how I felt at that point. I was alone, I knew that. And there'd been no communication with the outside world, because there was no radio or television, of course. No newspapers or magazines. I was still quite weak, and I felt no urgency to return to this world. I had a deeper need for the serenity I found there." She bit her lip, looking away from his openly skeptical gaze. "Before the plane crash I hadn't accepted that there was a lack in my life . . . but deep down I knew there was. I had to find out what it was, and why it was there." She frowned, realizing by his scowl that she'd hurt him, that he didn't understand. "I mean, there was so much of my life I'd let slide. I'd given over control of it to others and had made myself needlessly unhappy by doing so."

"Thank you for that," he said tightly. His chest hurt with what she'd said. There was truth in it, though. Maybe if they'd talked . . .

She shook her head. "I'm not blaming anyone but myself. It began when I was young. It was easier to take the down path than struggle with the up one. I'd done the minimum amount of work in school. I could've worked harder at painting and sculpting, but it was easier to let it slide. So I did. At the lamasery I learned there was a good deal to be absorbed if one was willing to probe. I began to paint, really paint, and sculpt. Once I got started it was like I'd been starved and was now in a feeding frenzy. I couldn't stop. I just kept turning out more and more work. It helped me to open up, to look inward, to find out who I was. Can't you see, Cas? I was getting well in every way. I couldn't abandon that until I had let it fill my life." She paused, licking her dry lips.

"Go on." He didn't want to hear, but he had to know it all, even if her words were like hot spears through his flesh. Margo! Alive! His greatest dream come true. Now, he wasn't sure if he could handle it.

She reached for a water jug on the side table, her hand trembling as she poured herself a glass. She took two big swallows before continuing. "Months before I was ready to leave, one of the lamas took a few of my paintings to Lhasa, to try to sell them for me, since I had no money to pay for the cosmetic surgery I was going to need. All of them were bought by the agent of a wealthy

Japanese businessman, and he became my patron of sorts. He opened doors for me in Europe and here in New York. As my paintings and sculptures began selling in a few galleries in both London and Paris, I began to believe that I could reenter my old life, on my terms, knowing who I was, being productive, paying my own way—"

"Qi—Margo, whoever the hell you are, you had money," Cas broke in angrily. "You could have had any amount you wanted, not only from me, but from Ivor as well." He angrily slapped his hand against his bare thigh, then looked down, as though suddenly remembering he was still naked. He reached for his crumpled shirt, slipping it on and buttoning it with shaking hands. "There was no need for you to work for your money. But as you say, you wanted to control your life, and you did. I have to wonder what brought you back here."

Stung, she stared at him. "My life is here."

"Is it?"

"Yes, it is," she flung back at him, her anger almost matching his.

"You've had your fun tonight."

Anger died as quickly as it had risen. "Yes, I did have fun tonight. And I hope you did," she added. "I enjoyed every minute of it. We talked, we danced, we were really alone and we communicated."

Her words were like tiny stabs. His mouth tightened. "You're intimating those things weren't in our marriage."

"Were they?" She held her breath. It wasn't as easy as she'd thought it was going to be. The relaxed camaraderie between T'ang Qi and Cas Griffith was slowly eroding. Fear churned in her stomach.

"Damn you!" he exclaimed. "I was happy in our marriage." He hauled in deep, painful breaths. "We loved each other." He ignored the niggling voice deep inside him, reminding him that he'd had the same feelings about the barriers in their life. But hot anger was throbbing through him, and he wouldn't allow himself to see any side but his own. He'd damn well been to hell and back without her!

"I know we loved each other." The tenuous hold she had on happiness was sliding through her grasp. "But can't you see that in many ways we hid from each other? That we needed more?" She shouldn't have said anything, she thought. Stupid woman. Anything was better than losing Cas. But the die was cast. Like Julius Caesar, she'd crossed her Rubicon. Her life demanded truth. Their relationship would crumble without it. Their love would be eroded by anything less. Yet would it last with it?

"We had it all," he said tautly, knowing that he lied as he said it.

"We had great love and great lovemaking." She exhaled a shaken breath. "Our love needed more. We didn't communicate—"

"I looked for you." The anger within him turned sour. How dare she question him about their love? Needed more! The fact that she'd verbalized what he'd thought over and over again didn't mitigate his fury. It enhanced it, gave it an aura, a presence. Now it couldn't be hidden. The ghost of

real feeling didn't dance around their lives anymore. It hung between them and it wouldn't go
away.

She'd abandoned him to better herself! She'd
known he loved her. She had to know that he'd
have taken the Himalayas apart with a teaspoon
if he'd thought there was any chance of finding
her. She must have sensed his agony when her
remains had been returned to him. He damn near
went out of his mind! He remembered his horror,
how he couldn't believe her gone, the raw night-
mare of having to identify the remains of what
was thought to be her body and some of the frag-
ments of unburned clothing that clung to it. It
had been pure, unadulterated hell, and he'd
drunk himself to sleep for months afterward.

"I looked for you," he repeated in an agonized
whisper.

Margo dropped the sheet and leaned toward
him. "I'm sure you did. Can't you understand
that I was fighting for my life for long, pain-filled
months? That I didn't know who I was, let alone
who you were, for agonizing weeks? The only
thread to my sanity, the lifeline to my struggle to
live, was my mentor. Without him I would've died.
Many times I thought I was already dead." She
hauled in a shaky breath, not telling him how
often she'd screamed for death when the pain had
been too great.

He shuddered as though her pain had entered
his body and he could feel his skin burning. God!
She'd been so badly hurt. "There were no phones,
no way for someone to get a message to me?" he
asked. Frustration ballooned in him; he felt her

pain, but he battled his own. He'd damned near died with wanting her back. Now, she was here, and he couldn't handle it. Maybe dreams weren't meant to come true. He was stung with sensation, bleeding from every pore. Finding her was as shattering as losing her.

"There were no phones," she answered, "but yes, messages can be sent from the lamaseries. Yet months passed before I was able to deal with my broken body. Pulling myself together was agonizing . . . arduous . . . accomplished inch by inch. And I had to use every atom of my being to do it. I knew I was assumed dead. The lamas who'd found me had told me there'd been no other survivors. So I concentrated on trying to find my way back to good health of mind, body, and spirit. Months of therapy were required." She looked up at him. "When I recalled who I was, I remembered you first. I wanted to get back to you, but I had no strength."

He stared at her. The barely noticeable facial scar took on monumental proportions. He felt stabbed to the heart. "Margo! Dammit!"

She saw tears in his eyes as she swiped at the ones on her cheeks. "There were no sophisticated drugs, you see, and I couldn't tolerate the opiates they had. Some of the herbs helped, but mostly I had to concentrate on self-hypnosis to alleviate the pain." She laughed shakily. "Sometimes my concentration wasn't good enough."

"God, darling, I—" All the loneliness, her personal hell, his own bereavement, stabbed him like ragged swords.

"But I was beginning to learn," she added hurriedly. His distress hurt her. "At first learning was a distraction, and I didn't really take anything in. But after a time I began to discover myself as a person. Many of the holes in my life were gradually filling with scholarly pursuits. Those were things I'd thought alien to my life. That wasn't true. I'm a good student, and I'm accomplished, and that all happened because I needed to be distracted from my illness and the pain. Learning became a great panacea. It all but pushed me back to health. All that time I struggled to get well could've borne down on me like another burden. Instead, with the help of others, I found a new facet of my life, allowing an all-but-latent talent to bloom. Now, I'm an artist."

"I know. And your reputation is growing," Cas said slowly. It tore at him to remember how she'd said nothing to Ivor or to him when they'd asked her what she wanted to do with her life. Or had they asked? Had they simply strongly suggested the route she should take? He was uncomfortable all at once. Had she just gone along with his plans for their honeymoon, not really enjoying herself? And Nepal! His heart wrenched within him. He'd all but insisted she go, and he'd regretted that a thousand times. God, he'd all but carried her on the plane.

He studied her. Her face had been radiant as she explained her road back to recovery, and how her art and zest for learning had been reborn. He'd never seen that inner fire before. Jealousy struck him, and he hated that. He'd never been jealous of Margo. He might've been possessive. . . .

"You're a poised, successful woman now," he said.

She nodded. "I am. And I like being that way. Before, I was schooled. Now I'm educated, and I'll continue that education until I die. The lamas showed me that we can never learn enough, and they showed me that learning can save a life. It saved mine, and my sanity. When I thought I'd go out of my mind with pain and anxiety, the lessons calmed me, salved my weary mind and spirit. My vistas widened, my hunger to know more increased every day."

She paused when he backed away another step, as though what she told him hurt. "Cas, listen to me. I had to continue for the health of body and mind. And as my spectrum widened, I began to know myself more. With that knowledge came wellness. It brought me self-confidence. I knew I would live, and I knew I had the ability to explore different avenues that opened up for me. By the time I was really well, I was eager to come back to you, but I needed to face you. So, I didn't send a message to anyone." She hesitated. "I didn't know if you'd have believed it was me if I phoned."

Should she describe how frightened she'd been, wondering if he'd remarried, or if he'd flat out deny her?

"When I was finally well enough to travel," she continued, "I wanted to come home. But my patron had set everything up for me with a plastic surgeon in London."

"I wouldn've flown there," Cas said abruptly.

She sighed, nodding slowly. "If you'd been able

to accept what I said over the phone, I know you would've. But can't you understand that I needed to face you, to see your expression, to explain. Besides, once I was in London, I was catapulted into the medical procedures. After the operation there were follow-up visits and more therapy, which took a great deal of time. I was coming home as fast as I could, but I couldn't be foolish about my convalescence. And all along the way I was shoring up a crumbling, pathetic part of me."

"You were never pathetic," Cas said harshly. "You were loved and cherished. You had a life with me, with our families. We needed you." He didn't dare say how much he needed her. It had been a nearly lethal blow to realize how empty his life had been without her, how gray and drab his existence. Qi had shown him that. But there was no T'ang Qi. Or was there no Margo? He was hiding from her again, the one thing he said he'd never do. How damned hard it was to open up. "I needed you."

"I know, because I needed you," she said softly. He'd shied away from saying he loved her, she thought. That hurt. "'Cas, I love and cherish freely now. I don't hide anymore. Nor do I put on a happy face and say nothing when things annoy and upset me. I speak my mind, say what I feel. I try not to hurt other people's feelings, but I know I have a mind and opinions and I'm not afraid to show them."

Cas blinked, surprised to hear her speak his thoughts. He felt raw, intensely vulnerable, exposed. "I'll say what I'm feeling too," he said at last. "What do you want me to call you?"

Margo shrugged, trying to quiet the dread building in her. Cas might think he was open with her, but she could feel doors shutting in her face. "Either Qi or Margo, or both. It doesn't matter. My name is a mere label. The real me is a soul of great worth. It doesn't need a name." She paused. "It needs love."

"Don't we all," Cas muttered. He sank down on a satin-covered boudoir chair. "Now what?"

"I must contact Ivor."

"Kind of you to think of him," he said tartly.

"You're a bit acidy, aren't you?" She studied him, unwinding a bit that he'd sat down and not stormed from the room. She stretched forward on the bed, cupping her chin in her hand, almost relaxed, and certainly happy to be with her husband.

"You weren't always so uninhibited . . . in the light," he said, his gaze running hungrily over her, almost against his will. "When the lights went out, it was different." They'd been wild together. His anger didn't die, but it abated. He couldn't fight the happiness of having her back with him.

She laughed. "I remember. Now I don't need to turn out the lights unless I choose."

"Is that right?" He studied her closely. She was more beautiful. She was exquisite. Her voluptuousness was gone, but there was a tight sexiness to her, a raw sweetness that was overwhelmingly appealing.

"You're my husband," she said. "Why should I

be embarrassed?" She rose and stood on the bed, gloriously naked. "I could show you a few moves in t'ai chi, if you like." She curled her arms in sweeping circles, then turned rigid, taking the stance.

"I saw your moves when that hooligan approached you outside the gallery," he said hoarsely, not able to take his eyes off her. She was Venus. Her calves and thighs were smoothly muscled, and there wasn't an ounce of excess flesh on them or any other part of her body. Her breasts were firm, tilting upward, smaller than they'd once been, but no less sexy. Her face amazed him. It was the same, yet there was a delicate heart shape to it that he didn't remember. His body hardened.

Margo smiled down at him, letting him see that she was fully aware of his arousal. "You're a very sexy man."

"And you're a voluptuary." He rose and went to her, pulling her into his arms, pressing his face to her breasts. "I'll never let you go again. Never." Had another man taught her to be so uninhibited? he wondered. No, he wouldn't dwell on that. He'd had enough women. He had no right to ask her anything. Besides, she controlled her own life now. Acid mirth trickled through him. There was a great deal unresolved between them, but it was too mind-boggling to juggle it all now. Right now he wanted her again.

She gasped when he swept her up into his arms, then dropped to the bed with her, cushioning her fall with his body. "I think I'll like making love to you in the light, wife."

"Me too," she murmured, her body arching as he caressed her. Moans and gasped rolled out of her. The loving violence of his caresses spun her into a wild vortex. She'd never experienced such a flood of love. Embracing him tightly, she tried to let him know how she felt about being back with him. When his tongue trailed from her chin to her belly, she went limp with delight.

He caught her close, sliding up to face her. Their eyes met. "I'm going to make you hot and wet for me," he murmured.

"I think I already am." She let out a little scream when his tongue entered her body, initiating a fierce cadence that had her thrashing on the bed. "Cas!"

"I'm with you, sweetheart." Blood thundered through him as he moved back up her body. He couldn't get his breath. Hot, sweet delight pierced him as she licked his face, his neck, his chest. "I'll never let you leave me."

"I'll never want to go," she answered, but wondered if he heard her. The irresistible passion was on them and it blew them apart, fragmenting them, sending them beyond the stars.

The lovemaking was sweet, wild, wonderful. They went slow and then fast, turned and twisted on the bed. They gave and gave.

It was all Margo had remembered. It was all the heat and light she needed for living. It was much, much more than it had been the first time, and she reveled in the passion, giving all of herself to it. If in the back of her mind she had the uneasy feeling that Cas had not quite come to terms with her return, she smothered the black discomfort. But all the lovemaking in the world could not bury the resentment, the questions, the anger.

Six

The trouble started the next evening when Margo told Cas over dinner that she was looking into leasing a studio in Soho.

"Soho!" he exclaimed. "Are you out of your mind? That's a high-crime area. I won't have my wife put at risk."

Instantly defensive, she glared at him. "You're not my feudal lord, so stop the grand-seigneur act. I don't like it."

"I'm not acting!" he yelled.

"I have a career, just as you have," she said, striving for calm. "I need to have a place to work, just as you have your office. I won't be smothered."

Hurt flashed across his face, and she could've bitten her tongue. Was she being arbitrary? she wondered. It hadn't been her plan to alienate Cas, only to let him know that she wanted to pursue her life, just as he did his, without damaging what they had together. "Cas . . . maybe I'm not being clear on this—"

"Oh, I think you're crystal clear, wife." He bit off the words as though they were chunks of steel, then refused to discuss the issue further.

If Cas minded that she spent her entire day in the studio—and she often left in the morning before he woke up, needing that relatively quiet time to soothe her spirit—or that she usually unplugged her phone while there, not wanting to be disturbed, he never said. If he minded that she was making new acquaintances in the art world, people he didn't know and who shared with his wife a talent that he could scarcely comprehend, he kept silent. Too often, the air between them vibrated with tension, as Margo determinedly pursued her new life, and Cas tried to fathom the woman he'd married.

One evening, a month after she returned, Margo stood in her bedroom contemplating her marriage. She and Cas weren't like long-lost lovers craving each other's embraces. They were more like circling wolf-pack leaders, waiting for an opening to go in for the kill.

She sighed, smoothing her hands down the front of her dress. It was their first evening entertaining at home since her return, and she didn't relish it. She and Cas needed more time alone before they could tackle outsiders. But maybe it was best to get it over with. Though she'd seen Ivor and Ione several times, she hadn't seen Cas's parents—who'd been on vacation in Greece—or his brothers. It had to be done. When she'd spoken to Celia and Weldon on the phone, she'd sensed a measure of hostility. Even Ivor and Ione, after recovering from the initial shock and happiness, had been disgruntled from time to time. Margo shook her head. No need to dwell on that now. She and Cas and the trouble between them were all she could handle at the moment.

Sighing, she glanced around her bedroom. One wall of the room was mirrors. Behind them were the sliding doors to her mammoth closet. Cas used the closet in the adjoining bedroom of the master suite. Sometimes she felt so alone. Not that she slept alone. Each night Cas came to her bed and they made love. Sighing again, she faced the mirrors and tried to concentrate on how she looked. Some things, besides the great sex, hadn't changed in their relationship. The communication between them hadn't resolved itself in quantum leaps—nor even in baby steps. Were they any further ahead? Maybe if she didn't go to the studio so much, maybe if he didn't work such long hours, even though he worked at home much of the time, maybe, maybe, maybe.

She studied her image, turning first this way and that. Western clothes still felt somewhat alien to her, and certainly not as comfortable as the cheongsasm that she'd grown accustomed to wearing. It should have been fun shopping for all the clothing and accessories she needed. The cloud hanging over her marriage changed that.

"You look lovely."

She whirled around and smiled at her husband. There was still a measure of wariness, but she was determined to whittle it away. She wouldn't even consider that they might not come to trust each other fully, and in a short time too. Her insides spun in tight circles at the idea of losing him. She couldn't live without him again.

Her painful thoughts must have shown on her face, for Cas swiftly crossed the room to her, frowning in concern.

"Are you all right?" he asked, unable to keep from staring at her. She was a vision in pale jade, with jade earrings dangling from her earlobes. She was a jewel, and he wanted her desperately. He wanted her all the time!

He worked more at home now than at the office so he could be with her whenever she wasn't at her studio. He was becoming adept at running his company from home and delegating authority. The business that had consumed him since the plane crash had now been shoved to the back of his mind. His staff was highly motivated, surprised and eager that he should hand over so much of the work to them, leaving him free to focus on his wife and his life with her. Yet her focus seemed to be on her art, on establishing her independence. He was happy, he constantly told himself, but he wanted more. They made love every night, monumental, consuming passion that wore him out and strengthened him as nothing ever had. But there was more to be had and he knew it. He needed it. In many ways it was as it had always been, but now the barriers were like slivers under the skin. They had to be taken out to let the healing begin. More times than he could count he'd catch her gaze on him. He sensed a

disappointment in her, and answering frustration bloomed in him. He could conquer mountains in the business world, but he couldn't
approach his wife. He wanted to think there was
better communication, and in some ways there
was, but they still skirted issues. Talk. That's
what they needed to do. But even when they did
that, there was a hesitancy, a hedging.

And, he admitted, he was jealous about the two
years she'd spent without him. He knew little
about her mentor, or the people she'd been close
to in Tibet. He avoided asking her about that
time, yet he wanted to know. Had she loved anyone then? He was overly aware that she never
asked about the women he'd seen when she'd
been gone. He wanted to tell her, explain about
the hell where he dwelled in garish, plastic
splendor.

Margo frowned as she studied Cas's face. He
was in his own little world again. It was a tortured world, just as hers had begun to be. It had
been so simple to slip back into the easy role of
doing and saying nothing that would upset the
apple cart. It annoyed her that she'd done it. It
wasn't that they didn't converse. They did. He
talked about his day, she told him about hers.
Neither opened up the can of worms of the past,
though. She knew there'd been other women in
his life. That had been difficult enough to deal
with. She didn't know if she could accept it if
he'd loved one of them, or still did. She avoided
the question, yet she knew that such things had
to be brought out into the open. Would they ever
get off the seesaw relationship they had?

"Shall we go down?" she said lamely. "The others will be arriving soon."

Cas nodded, reaching into his pocket. "I have something for you." He hesitated when he saw surprise flash across her face. "Do you mind that I'm giving you a gift?"

"No. I just didn't expect it." Her heart fluttered in her chest. He was her man, he'd given her a gift. All at once she felt girlish, bubbly.

He smiled. "Get used to it, love." He wanted to wrap up the world and hand it to her. He wanted to love her everywhere and all the time.

He called her love! she thought giddily as he handed her a small, flat box wrapped in silver paper.

"Open it," he said.

Cas was excited. Being near her did that. That she was somewhat less than her serene self mitigated the irritation he always felt at the power she had over him. He was beginning to know the new Margo, maybe better than the old, even if they still wore masks with each other. From their first meeting at the art gallery, she'd been friendly and open with him, but he'd seen the hesitations behind her smile at times. Now and then she'd seemed far away, almost mysterious, as though there was a part of her he could not see.

Yet then, he mused, he'd thought he'd known his wife two years ago. He was sure now that Margo had hidden much from him then. And honesty forced him to admit that he'd done the same with her.

Honesty, he thought with a bit of distaste, was no easy thing. When the new Margo, his wife of almost two years who was a relative stranger, confessed to him one evening while they dined that she'd thought their honeymoon a marathon of sorts, he'd been shaken to the core. Guilt had risen like a flood, even though he was certain she hadn't meant that to happen. But if he'd taken her home when he'd had to go, then she wouldn't have been on that plane. . . .

"I would rather have gone home," she said, "than continue all the skiing we did. Three weeks away was ample. When it turned into a six-week marathon, it all began to blur." Cas could still taste the sourness of his surprise and hurt. In that way she was the new Margo. Most of the time she didn't hold back. She vented her feelings. But he wasn't fooled by her plain speaking. There was a part of herself that she husbanded carefully. She still kept secrets. Margo of the mobile features had become Margo of the inscrutable oriental outlook. She was open but closed, frank but secretive. She'd told him she wanted to be more open. He found that laughable. If anything, she was less open. Adept as she was at hiding her feelings, he couldn't often see a reaction to what he said or did. He could now, however. Her trembling hands gave her away. She was not as unaffected as she appeared.

She unwrapped the silver paper and lifted the cover of the velvet-lined box. "Oh," she said, taking a deep breath. "It's jade . . . and old. Isn't it?"

He nodded. He'd searched the city for the cream-colored jade pendant with the dragon carved into its surface. "It came from northern China. I thought you'd like it."

Tears sprang to her eyes. "How thoughtful. I love it."

"Do you remember Crispin?"

"Yes, he designed my engagement ring." She smiled sadly. "That beautiful ring is somewhere in the snows of the Himalayas."

"I'll get you another ring, darling. I want to get you another wedding ring anyway." He bent down to kiss her.

She touched his face with one finger. "I don't need another engagement ring, but a wedding band would be nice."

He turned his head and took her finger into his mouth, beginning to suck, his gaze on her.

"We have guests," she whispered. She pulled her hand back reluctantly, her heart beating hard at the hot look in his eyes. She wanted him fiercely. "So," she said with effort, "tell me what Crispin said about the jade."

"It's old, as you said. But he considers it a one-of-a-kind piece, probably made as a specialty gift for a lady centuries ago." He was surprised when she lifted the lavaliere from the box, then turned so he could fasten the fine gold chain around her neck. "Does it go with your outfit, Margo?"

"It will have to. I intend to wear it all the time," she said simply. "This is Chinese jade. It brings wisdom and good luck. It must be worn forever." She smiled over her shoulder. "Thank you."

He flushed with pleasure. When she turned back around to show him how she looked, he nodded, then caught her in his arms. "You're beautiful."

She leaned back a trifle and stared up at him.

"So are you. And after your family leaves tonight, we'll talk about that." She held her breath until he nodded slowly, then reached up to kiss him. When he reacted at once, his body hardening against her, she pressed against his shoulders, pushing him back.

"Company." She put one finger on his lips when he bent toward her again. "Can't do it."

"To hell with the company," he growled, irritated at the thought of the long evening of entertaining ahead of them. "Tell them to go home."

She laughed out loud. "That's what I'd been thinking, but we can't. It's your family." She felt so sexy when he touched her. She wanted to lock him in a room and throw away the key. In fact, she'd been feeling so sexy the last few days, she could've followed him to his office and attacked him at his desk. On her honeymoon she would've said that it wasn't possible to love him more than she did. Since her return, her feelings had burgeoned, making those of yesterday pale by comparison.

"We'll see them another time," Cas said dismissively. He wanted her, to love her, to talk to her, to embrace her, to have her love him, embrace him, talk to him . . .

She paused, hearing something, then looked toward the door. She reached for his hand and curled her fingers through his. "We should greet our guests. I think they've arrived."

"Damn them all," he said softly, kissing the corner of her mouth. He needed her at that moment, painfully. "You give the jade life, beautiful lady."

Margo smiled, but the smile faltered as a strange sensation washed over her.

"What is it?" Cas asked.

"I don't know. I had the feeling my mentor was communicating with me." She shrugged, trying to shake off the fluttery sensation. "I can't explain it."

Jealousy rippled through Cas. He struggled against it, knowing her mentor was an elderly man. It didn't stop the green disease in his body and mind. Her life with her mentor had been one of openness and honesty, a deep commitment to learning and the betterment of the mind, body, and spirit. He wanted that with his wife. Why had it been so easy for her with a stranger and so difficult with him?

"We should go down," he said stiffly.

Margo paused, watching him. "Perhaps you'll accompany me to Tibet one day." She wanted that, though before it happened, their life would have to be on more solid ground.

Cas didn't respond. He simply took her arm and led her out of the bedroom. Once they were in the hall, they clearly heard the sounds of conversation and laughter.

Margo paused at the top of the steps to murmur her mantra. "Your brother Dean married while I was gone."

Cas nodded, leading her down the curving staircase. "Linnie's a nice girl. She might not have much good to say about me." He shrugged.

Margo stopped to face him. "Oh? Why is that?"

Before Cas could answer, her Uncle Ivor stepped out of the living room and looked up at them. "I wondered when you were coming down," he said gruffly, his arms opening wide. "Sometimes I just need to look at you, dear Margo. Then I can believe you're back with us." He frowned at her. "But we'll have to put some meat on your bones, and you mustn't work as hard . . ." His voice faded when she tilted her head to one side, her quiet gaze fixed to him. "You don't want me interfering."

Margo freed herself from Cas and hurried down the last few steps to her uncle. "I want you to remember that I'm strong, healthy, and able to do my work—and I love doing it. Art is my life's work."

Ivor nodded, then glanced at Cas, who was looking at his wife. "And does your husband approve of your loft in Soho? I think it could be dangerous."

Margo chuckled. "Don't try to armor your position with my husband, Uncle. It won't work. Cas knows I love painting and sculpting, and that I need my own place to work. I found it and intend to keep it."

Ivor nodded, but his glance slid toward Cas. Margo's husband was tight-lipped, flinty eyed. He didn't look as though he agreed with her. Ivor looked back at his niece. She stood straight and proud. His once shy, accommodating Margo was no more. But maybe he'd like this one even better. Certainly Ione more than approved of the new Margo.

He glanced again at Cas. There'd been a change in him in the last month. He looked younger. He'd all but lost that haunted visage, the gray emptiness. But . . . there was still a tautness there, a latent anger. Were he and Margo having trouble? "Do you think your wife works too hard?" Ivor asked Cas.

Cas's smile was tight. "She's an independent woman. She demands the career and personal autonomy that should belong to everyone. And she loves what she does. I assume she knows how to pace herself."

That his wife's very independence alienated Cas from time to time was something Ivor didn't need to know. That he had to struggle with a jealousy that had no rhyme nor reason was his own personal bête noire.

"She was very ill," Ivor said.

"But not dead," Margo said gently, then kissed her uncle's cheek. "Don't think of me as a child, Ivor. I'm a woman, and I like the woman I am."

Ivor blinked at her softly spoken bluntness. "Of course. Your Aunt Ione agrees with you." He looked again at Cas. The muscle jumping at the side of his mouth made a mockery of his seeming calm. Margo appeared not to notice that she was upsetting those around her.

"Perhaps we should join the others," Margo said, then added to her uncle, "Cas knows what I want, Ivor. He supports me."

A harsh question suddenly ripped through her mind. Had she supported Cas enough? He shouldn't have to make all the concessions. She gasped at that hard realization.

Cas put his arm around her waist and stared down at her. "What is it? Are you in pain?"

"Revelation is often painful," she said, smiling weakly.

"Well, then, come along," Ivor said gruffly, taking her arm. "You have guests." He led her ahead of Cas into the living room. "Here she is, Wel and Celia. Arthur, come see your sister-in-law." Ivor gestured to the youngest of the Griffiths, then looked at the other brother. "Dean, you must introduce your wife."

Margo greeted Cas's parents with a hug. She was not surprised, but was hurt nonetheless, that both were rather stiff with her. As with her aunt and uncle, they had aged noticeably in the past two years—Weldon had more gray hair, lines bracketed Celia's mouth—but they appeared healthy. She turned from them as Arthur approached, smiling easily at the charming young man.

"It's good to see you," she said as Arthur embraced her.

"I can't believe it, Margo." He stepped back to study her. "You're alive and well . . . and your husband's still very possessive of you." The irrepressible Arthur grinned at his tight-lipped brother. "Some things never change."

"No, they don't," Cas said softly, slipping an arm around Margo's waist. Seeing her in another man's arms—even when that man was his own brother—forcefully brought home to him just how much she meant to him. At the soonest opportunity he was going to tell her exactly that. Nothing, not her art nor his company nor any other person, was going to be allowed to get in the way of that. He would never let her go again.

"Some things I don't want to change," Margo said, laughing at the two brothers and feeling giddy when her husband's eyes darkened in passion. Hopefully, it would be a short evening, she thought.

Arthur looked her up and down. "Wow. You were always lovely, Margo. Now you're a knockout. Are there others like you in Tibet?"

Dean pushed past his younger brother, towing a doe-eyed blonde who blushed shyly. "Margo, you look wonderful." He hugged her. "I want you to meet Linnie. We've been married three months."

"How do you do," Margo said to the young woman. "You're a lucky man, Dean."

"Thanks. I think so." He smiled at his wife, then looked back at Margo. "So's my brother. You're even sexier and more beautiful than before, Margo."

Margo smiled, then moved away to talk with her parents-in-law.

Cas watched her for a moment, then muttered, "I feel as though I'm dancing around a familiar stranger. Well, if she's having so much fun, I think I will too."

"What? What do you mean?" But Ivor was talking to air. Cas strode across the room to the piano, then sat down and let his hands rove the keys. He began to sing a love song that he and Margo had danced to while they'd been engaged and had called "our song." The lyrics were simple, describing the love between a man and a woman. It was a song for a dimly lit nightclub and a twosome, a tad off the mark for a family gathering.

Conversation didn't die, but it did falter.

Dean and Arthur grinned at each other.

"Is he trying to seduce his wife with that song?" Dean drawled.

"Is he drunk?" Linnie asked worriedly.

Dean shook his head. "Doesn't do that anymore."

Linnie sighed. "I wish he'd given it up before our wedding. Putting Mr. DeLine in the punch bowl didn't set well with my folks."

Dean shrugged. "DeLine shouldn't have mentioned Margo. Cas thought she was dead then."

"He doesn't act like he loves her that much."

Dean nodded. "He does. And he'd tear down the walls of this building to get to her." He glanced at Margo, who was staring at her husband. "And I think she feels the same."

Ione had also noticed how her niece was gaping and walked over to her. "You know," she murmured to Margo, "if you handled Cas the same way you handled Ivor, it'd work better."

Margo didn't turn her head. "You could always read people rather well."

"I love you, Margo. I thought you knew that."

Margo clasped her aunt's hand. "I know. I fully intended to be open with Cas. I had time to practice what I'd say to him. Somehow it was easier to rehearse it than do it, though. Why can't I do it?"

"Do it at a time when you'll both be surprised by the interruption. If you get my drift."

Laughter spurted out of Margo. Her husband looked her way, smiling, but he didn't stop singing.

"I think I'll take that advice," Margo said softly.

"Go get 'em, tiger."

"Wish me luck."

"I always have."

Margo ambled over to the piano, positioning herself in her husband's full view. When he ended the song, she leaned toward him. "Do you know this one?" She hummed a few bars. Cas nodded and began to play. He'd forgotten how well Margo sang. Her throbbing alto voice had great appeal. She would never have sung such a bluesy love song in the old days. She would've demurred and deferred. Not now.

"Lord, Margo, you burn up the piano," Dean said as she launched into the chorus.

"Let her," Arthur said, then winced when his mother sailed up behind him, caught the interchange, and pinched his arm.

Cas couldn't take his eyes off his wife.

Ivor started toward the piano, muttering, his mien tight and purposeful. Ione waylaid him.

"Get me a drink, will you?" she said, lifting her glass to her husband's face. "I'm thirsty."

Ivor stopped, staring stony eyed at the glass, then at his wife. "Don't try to be funny, Ione. I know your game. You're interfering again—"

"So are you, my darling spouse. You're trying to run her life once more. And you said, more than once in the past two years, that if you'd only had the chance, you'd have changed your managing ways with her. Yet here you are, trying to manipulate again. And you damn well can't. She won't let you, and neither will I. I was a fool to let you get away with as much as you did during her formative years. I did Margo a disservice."

Ione nodded sharply, her glance sliding toward the piano. "She's wonderful, better than before, stronger, assertive, but just as sweet. And I love her." She looked back at her husband. "This is your big chance, Ivor."

"That love song is rather suggestive," Ivor blustered, "and the way they're looking at each other . . . They have company. It's unseemly. Look at poor Weldon. He's shocked."

"Pooh. He'll get over it. Just leave Margo alone. She thought it would be easy to reconcile with Cas, but they've had some tough times. Let them straighten it out." Ione smiled at Margo. "She's only trying to seduce her husband."

"What?" Ivor's offended bellow brought several pairs of eyes his way, though not Cas's nor Margo's. They were gazing at each other. "Ione, how can you—"

"Easily. They're madly in love and having problems. They need the space and time to work things out. It won't be easy. Leave them alone."

"Fine, but what has that to do with the song she's singing? I still think I should say something." Ivor winced at his wife's disdainful look. "All right. I want her to be happy." He sighed.

Ione watched her niece admiringly. "I used to hear her humming and singing in her room when she was a child. I always thought she could carry a tune."

"Carry a tune?" Ivor said indignantly. "She had a superb voice coach. She studied violin and piano—"

"Ivor, I know all that. We married before she went to school, so I was around for quite a bit of her life. You didn't know I was there." She tried to smile when she saw the shocked look on her husband's face. "Sorry. I thought I was handling it until we believed Margo was dead. Then you turned to me and I loved it. I guess I don't want to be shut out again."

"Ione, how can you say that! You talk as though I cut you out of my life when Margo was with us . . ." Ivor faltered, then grimaced and swallowed hard. "I didn't mean to do that." He shook his head and looked back at his niece. His face crumpled. "I failed both of you, didn't I?"

Ione put her arms around his waist. "If you can admit that much, it gives me hope." She looked up at him as he gazed at her again. "You didn't fail us, darling. You simply underestimated us. She'll always be with us, but she must live her own life. And I'll always be with you. And I'm going to continue to run my life, as you should run yours. Give me a kiss, you pompous sweetheart."

He kissed her, then sighed. "Maybe we'll go away for the weekend. I need to find you again."

"Sounds good. We'll talk about it. But now I'd like to listen to my favorite child sing. I take a great deal of pride in her talent, not to mention how delighted I am with the serenity she's achieved. Maybe we could take a trip to the lamasery someday."

"Ione, you're incorrigible." Though Ivor rolled his eyes, a smile pulled at his lips.

Margo was having all she could do not to laugh, even as she sang another throbbing love song. It tickled her that she could recall so many of the lyrics. She'd forgotten how much fun it was to sing around a piano. There were so many of life's experiences that she'd never shared with Cas. Because she felt so interwoven with him, because she loved him so much, had she assumed he could read her mind about her wants and needs? Had she stressed her own needs too much and not given space to his?

Cas saw a shadow cross her face and wondered what had caused it. Was she unhappy with him? Stay, Margo, he pleaded silently. He knew how important her work was to her, and even if he didn't like her studio in Soho, he tried to be understanding. He was proud of her. He wanted her to keep working, to be herself. But he wanted her with him all the time, and he couldn't have that. It would take a while to sort it out smoothly, but it would be done. He couldn't lose her again.

The song ended, and Margo gazed intently at Cas. What had made him frown? she wondered. Was he unhappy with their life together? Maybe it was time for her to make some concessions too. She wanted him to be happy. She loved him.

"Do you know this one?" she asked.

Cas listened to her humming, then nodded. It was a funny love song, laced with sweet innuendo. He smiled, shaking off his gloomy thoughts. When she winked, his heart dropped to his shoes. She was beautiful. Was she trying to seduce him? Lord, taking her to bed was such a joy. He'd put his itchy concerns aside. The important thing was that they communicated on one level, perfectly. The rest would follow. He tamped down the cynical inner voice that whispered, when?

At the completion of the song, Cas applauded with the others. As everyone began talking again, he pulled her close to his side. "Those were some beautiful love songs you sang, love. Were they just for me?"

"Of course, darling. I didn't realize you played so well."

"I guess we still have a few discoveries to make about each other." He hoped his look told her what he was thinking.

"Talking and loving, loving and talking. Those aren't bad things to do. We can take the time to do that." She loved his low laugh.

He loved the suggestive look in her eyes. He wanted to tell the guests to go home and to take his wife to bed. She was so damned sexy. "We'll make the time for it."

"Then you were getting the message."

"If it was to love you, I got the message."

Margo grinned. "Bright boy. I haven't turned around to check. Have our guests gone home? Is Uncle Ivor disgruntled?"

"Actually, he's trying to nuzzle your aunt," Cas said, lifting her hand to his mouth and letting his tongue score down her palm.

"Is he?" Margo willed her body to turn around. It didn't respond. It was too connected to Cas and what he was doing to her. "Lucky aunt."

"Dinner is served," the houseman, Dannler, said from the doorway. His eyes widened a fraction when he glanced at Ivor and Ione.

Ione winked at Cas. "The kitchen fascist has spoken," she said.

"Time to eat," Margo said lamely. Then she

turned back to Cas and spoke hurriedly in a soft voice, before she lost her nerve. "You know, Cas, I thought we'd try all those innovative ways of making love . . . after I tell you what I want for our future and you tell me what you want."

"I want you," he said seriously, the smile leaving his face. "I want to know what you think about everything, what you like, what you hate, what you want from life . . . and from me. And I want to love you."

"Sounds like an all-nighter." Margo could hardly breathe. They were beginning to unmask in front of a roomful of people! They were revealing their feelings, letting their uncertainties throb into the light.

"And maybe all day tomorrow," Cas murmured. He hadn't moved off the bench. As his mother crossed to the piano again, he rose. "What do you think about making babies?"

"Good Lord," Celia said, frowning. "Haven't you had enough of that with those love songs? Give it a rest."

Margo turned to her mother-in-law, laughing. "They were pretty well-known songs. I couldn't have shocked you."

"Your father-in-law just downed two double Scotches, no ice," Celia pronounced sourly. Then she glared at her son. "You are even less predictable sober than when you were drinking a bottle of whiskey at dinner every night, then driving like a madman to our place out on the island."

"You're joking." Margo's humor faded. "He didn't drink all that." Visions of twisted steel and dead bodies jumped into her mind.

"He did. He operated his business in a semi-inebriated state," Celia said in tight-lipped anger, as though the thought of what her son had been still rankled.

"Mother!" Cas saw how Margo seemed to pull in on herself. "That's nonsense and in the past."

"Nonsense? You also tossed our family lawyer out of your office, bodily, because you had a hangover." Celia warmed to her subject. "And I can't discuss Dean and Linnie's wedding without getting faint."

"The punch bowl." Margo nodded. "Ione told me about that."

Celia glared at her son, then at Margo. "I'm sure any children you might have will be highly allergic to alcohol."

"No, they won't," Cas said, "because I don't drink like that anymore. I don't have to." He eyed his wife uneasily. She had a wild, angry look to her. "Margo?"

"You really drank that much? Every day?" Temper filled her like bad fumes. She choked with it.

"I told you I drank to sleep." He stared at her with alarm. His cool, contained wife looked as if she'd inhaled a devil and that the nether world now controlled her actions. "Take it easy," he whispered, reaching out to take her hand.

"Take it easy?" Her shouted question had the other guests turning back from the dining room. "Me? I didn't spend the time apart carousing. I was trying to get well." Her voice rose by decibels.

"So was I," Cas said, irritation filling him. "Do you know what it's like to find out your wife is dead when you were the one who sent her on the journey?"

"Big deal!" Margo yelled back. What were the horrifying statistics about drunk driving? Lord!

Cas leaned down, his face close to hers. "You can bet it was a big deal." He'd damn near died without her. Death would've been welcome some days.

The other guests drifted back into the living room, watching the tableau unfolding between husband and wife.

Alarmed, Celia muttered placating phrases that were totally ignored. "We'd better get to the dining room. Dannler called us."

"You could've killed yourself drinking," Margo said loudly, smacking her husband on the chest with the flat of her hand.

"Calm down, Margo." Cas tried to take hold of her hand.

"I am calm, you—you—" She hit him again on the chest.

Ivor stared, his mouth slack.

Ione held her drink up to her husband's mouth. "Take a sip. Then you won't pass out. Let the games begin." She smiled.

Weldon emptied his glass, then muttered, "I don't understand any of this," over and over again.

Linnie nudged her husband. "I thought you told me she was so refined. I've seen peddlers at a flea market more 'refined' than that."

Ivor glared at Linnie.

Ione chuckled.

"You dared to risk your life like that?" Margo

shouted. "Drinking like a fool? Never sleeping? Working fifteen-hour days?" She hit him in the chest one more time.

"Ow. What's the matter with you? Of course I drank and worked. What else would you suggest to a man who's losing his mind?"

"Don't try to weasel out of this, you home wrecker!" She pushed her face up as close to his as she could get.

"I was suffering," he lashed back.

"Suffering? What do you think I was doing? Making a tapestry for the Smithsonian? You were out with women, carousing, bedding them, making an all-around jackass of yourself."

"I was trying to forget." Even to him it sounded lame.

"You were a boozer, a bounder, a womanizer," Margo said all in one breath.

Silence palpitated between the two contenders.

"You know," Arthur said cheerfully to Dean and Linnie, "Marriage wouldn't be so bad if the fighting was always like this. I thought it was mostly about checkbooks and drapes."

"Shh, I can't hear," Ione said irritably.

Celia, who'd moved to her side, glared at her. "How can you eavesdrop at such a delicate time?"

"I notice you never left the room, Celia. I wouldn't have missed this for the world. They call it renaissance, my dear, renaissance," Ione said gleefully.

"Oh, really, this is ridiculous. Lancaster! Margo! You have guests. Stop that caterwauling and come to dinner."

The two looked at Celia as though they'd never

seen her before, as though she'd dropped from another planet.

A red-faced Margo recovered first. She nodded once to Celia, then looked back at Cas. "Don't think this is the end of it," she said angrily.

"You can bet I don't. I've plenty more to say to you." He rubbed his chest.

"Hah!"

Side by side, chins high, eyes flashing, they strode across the living room to Celia.

"I think Dannler said dinner was served," Margo said loftily.

Ivor looked at his niece, then down at his wife. "Perhaps she needs therapy," he muttered.

"Nuts!" his wife said inelegantly. "I think she just found all the therapy she needs." Ione looked thoughtful. "Maybe I'll buy her some boxing gloves. She already knows t'ai chi. Maybe an archery set . . . or an Uzi."

"Ione, are you so insensitive?" Celia demanded icily as she followed the other woman into the dining room. "No doubt we'll have a divorce on our hands soon."

"Or a normal marriage, which among the people we know would be more bizarre."

"I like Cas this way," Weldon said musingly. "He's got color in his face. Doesn't look so gray now."

"His face looks like a tomato that's about to explode," his wife said.

Seven

The guests had left and Dannler had retired. The house was quieting. The whispers were fading.

Margo showered and put on a dressing gown . . . and waited. If he didn't come to her room, she was going to his. The clock ticking on the side table sounded intrusive, loud. Was the shower dripping? She was about to use the television remote to get some conversation in the room when the door to the sitting room opened and Cas entered, rubbing his wet hair with a towel. It was obvious he'd used the shower in the other bedroom of their suite. He hadn't wanted to shower with her, and she'd wanted him there . . . even if she was still angry. Just the thought of the many things that could have happened to him was enough to turn her queasy and faint. How could he have been so foolish! Her hands curled into frustrated fists. They'd begun to unmask. She didn't want any more hidden words, gestures, or happenings. She swallowed hard, but didn't look away from him.

"We still haven't finished our talk," she said.

"It wasn't a talk, it was a shouting match." Cas was irritated with her, but he could have laughed out loud as he recalled how she'd turned on him. A veritable tiger! His wife had many interesting layers. Not once in all the time they'd been married had Margo railed at him the way she'd done that night. In fact, he'd never had a hint of the kind of temper she'd shown.

"Call it what you will," she said. "I want to finish it. What do you want?" Her fingernails dug into the palms of her hands. He was going to know how she felt about his debauchery when she'd been in Tibet. He'd had no right! He belonged to her and he could have killed himself.

"Let's clear the air," he said abruptly, caught between chagrin and humor. He wanted to rail at her, but more than that he wanted to take her to bed and make wild love to her in ways no one had even thought of yet. He didn't say that, though, because he was pretty sure his wife would tell him that lovemaking had always gotten in the way of their communication. And he didn't want to hear it, even if it was true.

"This might take a great deal of time," Margo said. She saw the summer lightning in his glance. He might be talking smoothly, his words temperate and controlled, but that was a mask. "And we're done with hiding," she blurted, and took a step back when his face contorted with renewed anger.

Cas saw the move, the defensive glance, the

uplifted chin. He nodded sharply. "All right. We talk." He threw off the short toweling robe he wore, and his naked body glistened bronze in the soft light of the bedside lamp.

"Talk?" Margo salivated just looking at him. She wanted him desperately, she needed that hard, strong body against her. He was a beautiful man and she loved him. Was he trying to put her off? She couldn't think clearly when she looked at his naked body. "Maybe we should go down to the library," she suggested.

He turned to look at her, smiling slowly.

"I mean, it might be more businesslike if—"

"Get into bed, wife."

She stared at him, then nodded once. Removing her robe, but not her nightgown, she slipped between the sheets.

He climbed into bed next to her. When his leg touched hers, he turned to her. "Is it permissible to kiss you while we talk?"

She shook her head. A kiss! She wanted much more than that, right now. She hungered for him. "We'd never talk."

"All right. Go."

Margo inhaled a deep, shaky breath. "I'll probably forget every detail of what I want to say." She faced him. "I hate that you drank and drove, that you risked your life time after time. When Celia talked about how you handled your business, and I added that to all the tidbits I've heard about your exploits, I could've exploded with fear. Even realizing it was after the fact didn't mitigate my terror. Every type of accident mushroomed in my mind in seconds. I could picture you speeding, weaving . . . crashing, crippling yourself. I honestly don't care about the women. Well, I mean I care, but I understand . . . well, maybe not understand, but I can accept them. Well, maybe not accept but . . . Dammit, they happened and I can't reorchestrate the past." She blinked when she saw the red creeping up his neck. Was Cas embarrassed?

"I don't want you to accept my having other women," he said. "Because none of them would have been in my life if I thought you were alive, anywhere on the planet, anywhere in this universe." He leaned close to her so that their heads were on the same pillow. "I couldn't sleep, I couldn't rest. You were everywhere, in my mind and heart, in my work, yet I couldn't touch you because you were gone . . . dead. I needed you, but you were only in my mind. You bedeviled me day and night. So I drank to drive the devils away. It helped to anesthetize myself."

"You could've died." Margo trembled, not even aware when she caught hold of his hand and inched closer to him. A world without Cas wasn't real, it was a gray purgatory filled with regret. "My first conscious thought after the crash was of you. You pulled me back from death. I was running home to you. Can't you see how important you are?" She brought his hand up to her face.

One tear rolled down her cheek. Cas's throat tightened; he couldn't swallow. "I didn't really care about being alive, sweetheart. I didn't think about safety, or survival. It was stupid, but I was caught in a damned whirlpool. At first I even contemplated suicide. But I couldn't kill myself overtly, so I chose the slow way. When you don't esteem life, you jab at it, roll dice with it. I didn't care that much about living. A hangover every day is damned awful, but it wasn't the real pain. Waking up and realizing you were gone was the agony." Even now, talking about it, it cascaded over him, bringing back the horror. It washed through him in choking, gagging waves. He shook his head to banish the nausea of memory.

Tears streaming down her face, she stared up at him. "But if you'd died, then what would I have come home to? Emptiness. I would've struggled to live for nothing. The emptiness would've killed me. Without you . . . Oh, Cas, that would have been hell."

He looked down at their entwined hands. "I used to picture you back with me." He grinned ruefully. "Usually I had a bottle of whiskey in my hand, and I'd sit in my study staring at the wall, talking out loud to you, telling you all the things in my heart, how I felt about you and our life together." He glanced at her. "I opened up to you. I talked and talked . . . and I begged you to answer, to come back to me." His crack of laughter sounded loud in the stillness. "Then I'd get angry with you and storm up and down the room, shouting at you to come home to me. It was insanity and I knew it." He took a deep breath. "I knew that much of my pain came from regret. Not just that I'd sent you on the trip by yourself, but that we'd never sat down and had one of the long heart-to-heart talks I had with the walls every night."

"I'm here. Tell me now. I'm listening. And I want to know."

"And I'll tell you." He kissed her cheek. "Are you cold, darling?" He put his arm around her, cuddling her close.

"Not cold. Apprehensive. I realize how close we came to never having the chance to say these things to each other. It's frightening to think that without the accident we might never have removed our masks." She looked up at him. "When I was far away from you, it was all so easy. Close up, it's a different story. I want to do this, to know everything, and I don't want to. Crazy, huh?" She touched his smiling mouth with her finger.

"Not so crazy. I don't relish opening up, but I do agree we have to, or we risk losing too much." He stared into her eyes. "The women were many and varied, tall, short, curvy, pencil slim, a kaleidoscope of hair coloring. But they had one common denominator. None of them wanted a commitment or marriage, and neither did I." He could barely recall the faces, but that wasn't surprising. He'd been drinking heavily most of the time. "Sometimes I went to work in the morning with my evening clothes on, changing to a business suit in my office." He shrugged. "I hated to sleep. I had dreams." The dread of conjuring her up in the snow, naked, running, scared him witless, and he'd done that more than once. He'd chase her, but he'd never catch her. And she was cold and calling out his name. He'd wake up bathed in sweat, crying.

Margo smiled, not surprised when she felt more tears spill over. "A regular workaholic Don Juan."

She bit her lip. "I imagined you with other women, now and then, when I was all but through with my therapy and didn't have to dwell on getting well. My mentor used to tell me not to agonize over things I couldn't control, but my mind was fertile ground. Then when I read some New York papers on the way to London, you were there. On the society pages, in living color, draped over some gorgeous woman. You looked positively limp."

He grimaced, imagining Margo looking at that picture after not seeing him for almost two years. "I'll bet you hated it."

"To tell the truth, it was so good to look at you, it didn't register that you looked somewhat . . ."

"Debauched? Smashed?" he said, irony lacing his voice.

"I was going to say, less handsome than usual." She grinned. "Not your usual sexy, virile self, lover boy." Should she tell him she'd held the picture to her mouth and kissed it?

Reluctant laughter gusted out of him. "At least one of us is having some fun with this." He'd always wanted her to think the best of him, to be able to love and respect him. It was like a nettle under his skin to recall that tawdry picture, but he couldn't call back those times.

Margo leaned back, sighing. "Most of our conversations since I've returned have been serious, sometimes even cumbersome. But would you believe, I've been having a good time." She chuckled at the look of surprise on his face. "Even wrestling that would-be purse snatcher to the ground was not really unpleasant. I couldn't believe it when you didn't know me, even while the rational side of me said that it would have been easy not to know me after the reconstructive surgery I had." She touched her face, smiling when his mouth followed her hand.

"You didn't look like my Margo. Your face is heart shaped now and your features seem smaller, the cheekbones more prominent. Before your face was almost oval, your cheekbones all but hidden."

"Fat face." She grinned.

He squeezed her. "You weren't fat. You were gloriously voluptuous and I loved your body. Touching it and loving it were my greatest pleasures." He saw the uncertainty in her expression and cupped her face with his hands. "And I love it even more now. You're svelte, supple, beautiful, and your face is exquisite." He shook his head. "I never thought you looked oriental before. But you do have a touch of it now. Exotic, intriguing."

"I know what you mean about me. It's so strange. Sometimes I feel Tibetan, as though that time at the lamasery infused me with new blood, as well as attitudes and principles."

Cas inhaled. "I've been jealous of your mentor a few times." Saying the words was like pricking a balloon. Somehow T'ang didn't seem so threatening anymore.

"Well," she said, "then I guess I can admit that the women bothered me a great deal, and that I wanted to bash them and you."

Cas threw back his head and laughed, banging his head on the filigreed brass of the bedstead. "Ouch."

"Are you hurt?" Margo lifted her hands to his head, the blanket dropping away from her body.

"Huh?" Cas stared at the luscious sight of her wonderful body encased in sheer silk, her breasts straining against her gown. "Margo," he said, his voice cracking. He tried again. "I can't look at you like this and concentrate on conversation."

"I was getting a little tired of talking myself." She fanned her eyelashes at him. They'd opened the door and pushed it wider. Now she wanted her husband, and all the joy he could give her.

He gripped her shoulders. "There's something else I want to tell you before I lose myself in you, darling." Sweat beaded his body as he fought to tamp down his arousal for a little longer.

"What's that?" She was melting, her body liquid and wanting.

"I love you, Margo. I have since you dumped me off that cat on the Seven Seas Lagoon. I didn't want to go down to Florida, I didn't want to meet my family's friends. But I bless that day, and all our times together, the good and the bad, the right moves and the errors." He kissed her cheek. "I wanted a life with you then, and I still do now. Don't cry, baby. Please, don't cry."

"I don't know what's the matter with me. I'm probably pregnant." She hiccuped and laughed.

Cas chuckled. "That's what's making you cry all over my chest?" Not that he wouldn't want a child with her, but they'd discussed children and had decided to wait a few years. A child! With no trouble Cas had pictured a chubby little girl with a jet-hued topknot and laughing blue eyes. Damn, it was wonderful. The future was wonderful.

"Well, something's changed," she said. "Maybe my hormones have gone wacky. Maybe my system changed when I returned to America. I've never been such a weeper." She patted his chest, tugging and twisting his curling chest hairs. Then she leaned closer to gently bite his nipple. "I feel crazy." She heard him gasp. "Did I hurt you?"

"God, no, angel, keep doing what you're doing." Cas's head went back, his eyes closed. Her mouth on him drove him wild, and he wanted it so much. This was the heaven he needed and wanted in his life.

"I do like making love to you," she said dreamily, "especially now that we've talked. It's better, sexier." Her mouth coursed down his chest to his waist, then she lifted her head. "Have I told you that I think you have a great body?"

"I don't know. Maybe. Tell me again."

"Oh, I will." Her words slurred as the power of her husband filled her. She kissed his belly, then his hipbones, her mouth sliding back and forth across him.

Cas couldn't stop gasping. He'd never felt so enervated, yet so energized. Margo's touch was magic. He gripped her to pull her up his body, but she pushed his hands away, her mouth going lower. When she took hold of him, caressing him gently with her fingertips, he groaned. "No, no, Margo, honey . . . I can't . . ."

"Shh." She felt him quiver under her hands. She put her mouth to him, tasting him, the roaring in her ears all but drowning out the hissing sound of her husband reaching the end of his tether.

"No, dammit. I can't take any more." Cas swept a laughing, excited wife up his body, watching as the smile left her face when he fitted her to him, thrusting into her powerfully. "Revenge," he said huskily. Her gasping laugh was an even greater spur to his libido.

"Umm, have to get comfortable." She looked down at him through her lashes and undulated her hips. She never noticed the effect on him, because she became so excited herself, she was lost in passion. Feelings mushroomed in her in great wonderful waves. She was out of breath, blood pounded through her. "I . . . can't stop," she told him when he tried to slow her down, soothe her, quiet her, draw out the ecstasy. "Oh, Cas, Cas. It's so wonderful." Clenching her body around him, she threw back her head, taking all of him, wanting all of him. His thrusts into her had her spiraling out of control into the wide, wild ionosphere of sexual love.

Cas could no longer tell where he ended and Margo began. They were one in the crackling flames of sensual fire. Energy spun about them. Shooting stars exploded in their faces. There was only one world. Theirs.

"Margo!" Cas cried out. "I love you."

"And I love you. Forever."

Spent, exhausted, exalted, loved, they spun slowly back down to earth. They held each other for long moments, the music of their movements still with them, ringing in their ears, resounding in their blood.

"I keep thinking it can't get better, but it does."

Margo opened one eye. "What magic formula do you use?"

"You," Cas said lazily. "Maybe it was so good because we knocked down some of the barriers first. What do you think?" He ran his hand down her neck. He loved her skin.

Margo opened both eyes, feeling replete, complete. They'd begun one of the more important tasks of their marriage, cleaning out the secret cubbyholes, dusting the corners of mind and spirit so they could enter together into their love covenant. It wasn't easy, but it had a wonderful effect.

"I think it could have everything to do with it." She touched his face. "Oh, Cas, you make me so happy. Some day I want you to meet my mentor. I want you to know the man who showed me the road back to you."

He kissed her gently. "Whenever you want to go, we'll go."

"Soon." She yawned. "Oh, sorry. Thank you. Tired." Her eyes fluttered closed, a smile on her lips when her husband laughed and called her sleepyhead. "Can't help it."

The next day she woke to his kiss. "You're terrible," she said lovingly. "I have to get to my studio this morning. You've been an inspiration and I can envision a wonderful, modern copy of the sculpture of David, only this time the model will be you. I can't just romp in bed with you, no matter how good an idea that is."

"Really?" Cas could hardly get his breath.

She didn't pretend to misunderstand him. "Yes, I'm doing a sculpture of you."

"Do I get to pose for it?" His laugh was shaky. He felt her stiffen, the smile sliding off her face. "Do I?"

"Yes, yes, of course. I didn't think you'd want to, but you know you're welcome. . . ." She smiled at him shyly. Words couldn't express the joy she felt. "And you won't mind coming to the studio?"

"Oh, I'll still get a little paranoid about your being there at times, but I am proud of you and I want you to continue with your work, sweetheart."

"Thank you." She kissed him lingeringly, then pulled back and frowned. "But now, I have to get dressed."

"Come to the office and we'll lunch together."

"I'd love that, but I promised Ivor I'd have lunch with him." She looked up at him hopefully. "Maybe you could join me at my studio after that."

He read the sparkling message in her eyes. "Sounds good. But if I strip down, I might make the same request of you. Besides, you might not want to sculpt the aroused me."

She laughed, kissing him. "It sounds wonderful. That lunch will be so boring."

He scooped her out of the bed.

"Where are you taking me?"

"I'm dumping you in the hot tub. Then I'm going to let you have your wicked way with me."

"Shame on you. You're leering." She hugged him, kissing his neck. She was so happy. The world was a perfect place because Cas was in it. And he was hers.

Wet. Wild. Wonderful. That was making love in the hot tub.

Lunch was predictable. The Colony. Broiled sea bass. Mineral water with an orange slice floating in it. They had a relaxed lunch that caused Margo to smile often. Ivor was making such a determined effort to stop his bullying, to treat her with new respect.

After a light, but delicious meal, Margo rose and excused herself, saying, "I must get back to my studio. Cas is meeting me there. Believe it or not, he's agreed to pose for me."

Ivor looked up at her dreamy face, then grinned. "Changed days, indeed. I never thought to see Cas Griffith at an artist's studio. I may visit myself one of these days. Ione raves about the place."

"I'd love to see you in my studio." Margo suddenly thought of Cas's modeling for her. "Ah, perhaps you had better phone first, though."

Ivor stood up and kissed his niece, smiling fondly at her. "Be safe, my darling." His words were soft, sincere, and it was clear to Margo that he was thinking about how he'd lost her in the plane crash.

After freshening up, Margo got the doorman to hail a taxi for her.

She was soon ensconced in a cab, staring out at heavy traffic. At least it was moving, she thought. Muttering her mantra, she tried not to be too impatient. But the cars, buses, and cabs were all slowing. Was there a bottleneck? No, another red light. Just as the light turned green, a car travel-ing on the cross street sped through the intersec-tion. But the street was blocked with traffic on the far side, and he got stuck in the middle of Fifth Avenue. Horns blaring, cars tried to maneu-ver around him. Gridlock, Margo thought. Oh, Lord.

"Driver? Can we get through?" Margo asked.

"I think so, ma'am. Don't worry."

Margo nodded and sat back, breathing a sigh of relief as the cab inched around the stuck car. Then she saw the sports car.

The cabdriver cursed, and then the other car slammed into their rear right fender. The cab jerked as steel crunched, and Margo was thrown on the floor.

Cas walked into The Colony. He'd timed his entrance to coincide with what he hoped would be the end of Margo's lunch with Ivor. He spotted Ivor's head at once. Striding to the table, he frowned at the empty seat. "Where's Margo?"

"Cas! I didn't think you'd be here. Margo left already to meet you at the studio." Ivor frowned. "You must've just missed her. Wonder you didn't see her leave as you came in."

Cas didn't wait to hear more. He didn't even question his overpowering need to be with her. It happened a lot. Anytime he didn't know where she was, the fear that he'd lose her rose in him like a flood. Lose her! He strode back across the restaurant to question the maître d', ignoring the customers who were waiting to be seated. That awful empty feeling was beginning to swamp him again. There was no reason for it. He'd find her and she'd be all right and he'd feel stupid.

"You might ask the doorman about the direction Mrs. Griffith's taxi was—"

Cas nearly ran out of the restaurant. He pulled the doorman aside and questioned him tersely. When he pointed down the avenue, Cas whistled for a cab. Fortunately, an unoccupied one was just passing. He hopped into it before it fully stopped.

"I'm looking for another cab with a woman in it," he told the driver, then briefly described Margo and the route she would be following. He slipped a fifty through the money window. "There's another one if we spot the cab and get it to pull over."

The driver nodded, accelerating. "Don't worry, mac. If they're on Fifth, we'll find them. Be grateful it's one way. We'll be in trouble if they turn on one of the side streets."

Cas nodded grimly, his eyes flashing left and right. Hell, he had to find her. That damned empty feeling. Maybe someday it would go away. Goose-bumps rose on his skin. He'd find her. He had to. She was his life. Then he'd take her to her studio and both of them would be nude and he wouldn't be posing and she wouldn't be sculpting.

He saw a tangle of cars up ahead. Gridlock? Accident? Perspiration popped out on his forehead. He had his hand on the door, ready to run down the avenue.

"Take it easy, Mac," the driver said. "No need

to get out. It's not a bad accident. Another cab, and a little sports car. Tough luck. We might be able to get around them."

Cas slapped another fifty through the money window and was out of the taxi, running, scarcely aware of the honking and yelling from the cars trapped by the accident and attendant gridlock. He'd seen Margo's head. He was almost to her. Cars were easing around the two vehicles, some jumping ahead, anxious to get out of the knot of traffic that had everyone's teeth on edge. The cab door opened and Margo tumbled out almost at Cas's feet. Brakes screeched. Horns blew.

Margo heard her husband's voice and tried to pick herself up from the ground. "Cas? Darling, what's wrong?"

Cas caught Margo up in his arms. "Are you all right?" he asked, gazing intently at her.

"Yes, yes. Where did you come from? How did you find me? I was on my way to you."

"I couldn't lose you again. I thought you knew that." His body quaked with anger and fear, the images of her being crushed in an auto accident pushing reason from his mind. "I know you don't understand—"

"Oh, I do, I do." A sob shook her. "Maybe for the first time I do understand your pain, my darling. I love you so." She held on to him as he leaned in the window and threw some bills on the front seat. "Shall we walk?"

"Too far," he whispered. "I'll find another cab." And he did, almost at once. Once inside he pulled her across his lap. "I had to get to you."

"T'ang would tell you that you saw the accident,

that because our souls are entwined you can feel my future," Margo said, feeling happy, though also a bit guilty. Had she even guessed at the enormity of his love for her? She'd concentrated so much on how she felt about him that she'd almost missed the wonder of his love. "Darling, Cas, I love you," she whispered in his ear.

"You're my wife and my life," he said, not looking away from her, his hands going over her.

"I'm all right. Honestly." She didn't even try to move off his lap. She saw the sheen of tears in his eyes, could feel the tremor in his hands, the thunderous beat of his heart. "Not a mark on me, coach."

"You could've been badly hurt," he said hoarsely.

"Not a chance."

He pulled her close, burying his face in her hair. "I knew something was going to happen, and I was damned scared. I still don't know why I felt I had to get to you. I was sitting at my desk thinking about you, trying to eat the sandwich my secretary had brought me. But even the coffee she made, and I generally like it, had a bitter taste. I couldn't swallow the bread. I felt queasy, threatened. It was as though something was telling me to get to you, and to hurry. I had to find you." He managed a smile. "My sandwich is probably still scattered across my desk."

"No doubt." She pulled back from him, caressing his face with her fingertips. "Darling. Didn't you know we're connected? Closely? You got the vibrations. You knew I was headed for trouble before I did."

He tucked her head down on his shoulder. "I should take you to the hospital."

She lifted her head, not sure whether to laugh or chide him. "I'm not going to the hospital. I'm going to the studio and you're going to take off all your clothes. Whee!"

He looked at her blankly for a moment, then a twisted grin appeared. "I was worried."

"I know." And he loved her. Margo was limp with delight. When they reached the studio, she was going to tell him and show him just how much she loved him.

Margo couldn't believe how delightful it was to make love with the lengthening day casting its light through the northern floor-to-ceiling window. If she hadn't wanted to keep their love life so private, she might have cast the image of their entwined bodies in bronze. She certainly had ample models to draw from as they made love again and again.

She touched neither brush nor chisel that day. Her hands were too busy with her man.

Eight

Margo stared at herself in the mirror and grimaced. No doubt she'd begin to show soon. She was between six and eight weeks pregnant, the doctor said. She sighed. Wonderful. Everything was fine. She and Cas would be parents. A miracle. Ione had guessed when they'd lunched together two days earlier.

"Dearest, I couldn't be happier. Ivor will be over the moon." Ione grinned. "Just think, me a grandmother. Of course it should be great-aunt, but I'm insisting on grandmother. And I like the feeling." Then Ione chuckled. "Celia will choke. She doesn't consider herself old enough to be one."

Margo touched her aunt's hand across the table. "Please, don't tell her, not yet." At her aunt's raised eyebrow, she shrugged. "I'd like to tell Cas first."

"What? You haven't told him? Dear one, you

must. You're so slender you'll show soon. Why haven't you said anything? Does it have something to do with that accident you had last month?"

Margo nodded. "In a way. He worried so much about me, I even agreed to see a doctor. I understand his feelings, Aunt Ione. He went through so much after the air crash, he just doesn't handle even slight accidents very well. In time that will change." She tried to smile.

"But you're worried about telling him about the baby."

Margo sighed. "It's silly, I know. But Cas seems withdrawn again, as though he can't let down his guard or something else could happen. He seems to brood. He says he's handling it, but he can't seem to let go." The smile slipped off her face. "It's as though he's wearing a new mask, and I can't get through to the other side."

Ione shook her head. "I suppose we shouldn't be surprised. Dear child, you've no idea what he was like when you were gone and we all thought you dead. He was a madman. I didn't see him that much, but when I did, he was never sober. And his eyes! It was like looking into the twin wells of hell. I marvel that he handled his company so well, and I assume he did because Weldon would've spoken to Ivor if something had been wrong. Celia despaired of him living more than a year. I've never seen her more distraught. No one could get through to him. It's not that he didn't try to get on with his life. He did, and through work. He kept a killing schedule and his social life was just as much of a burnout." Ione rolled her eyes. "He was constantly in the tabloids."

Margo nodded. "I know about the women. And he said he didn't sleep."

"I'm sure he didn't. He was like death." Ione paused, tapping one saberlike nail against her chin. Then she studied her beloved niece. "Why not take him to Tibet? Oh, not now, but after the baby's born. Let him see where you crashed, where you stayed, where you healed. I think he needs the therapy." Ione leaned over and squeezed her hand when she saw tears in Margo's eyes. "Hey, I know it's normal to be weepy when pregnant, but you'll wilt the lettuce if you continue."

"Heaven . . . forbid," Margo said, hiccuping and smiling. Tibet! T'ang! The quiet, the beauty of learning, the introspection . . . the healing.

"I'll be glad to take care of the baby," Ione went on, "along with the battery of nurses you'll have, of course. Diaper changing isn't in my job description. But I'd love to have the little blighter in my hands for a while."

"With all the attendants you need." Margo saw the eagerness masked by smart repartee and smiled. Ione would be a doting grandmother. Margo nodded slowly. "Maybe Cas does need that trip. Sometimes I forget just how much he went through."

"And he needs to know that the pain you suffered was not intended as a hot spear aimed for his middle." Ione nodded seriously when Margo chuckled. "I mean it, the man was tortured."

"Are you the Great One, Aunt?" Ione had always been able to see beyond facades.

"If you mean Confucius, the answer is no, but I do find his common sense comforting. I read a great deal of the Great One after you crashed." Ione reached out and squeezed Margo's hand.

Both aunt and niece held hands and shed a tear.

Now, looking at herself in the mirror, recalling her aunt's words, Margo decided that it was time to open another window into her life with Cas. First, she'd get his attention. She critically studied her outfit. Lounge pajamas in a satin-finished silk, the deep coral hue giving her skin a pinky luminescence. The color shone into her hair, enhancing the auburn highlights. From her jewelry chest she removed a coral rope that she twisted around her neck, and coral earrings mounted in filigreed gold that dangled almost to her shoulders. One more thing to don, and she'd be ready. Cas would be home in twenty minutes.

She glared at the handmade Italian slides with four-inch heels. She'd probably break her neck. For almost two years she'd worn little else but flat slippers. Margo sighed. Ah, well, she needed the effect the heels would give her. Putting them on, she rocked a bit, then the soft leather seemed to form around her feet like gloves. Taking a deep breath, she turned and glided toward the full-length mirrors on her closet doors.

"Wow, they do make a difference. I didn't believe Ione," she said softly, recalling how her aunt had all but forced her to buy the sophisticated footwear. She touched a little perfume to her knuckles and donned a coral ring on her right hand, took a breath, and left the bedroom.

Going down to the kitchen, she shivered in relief that Dannler had retired to his quarters at the back of the apartment. She didn't relish standing inspection in front of the canny houseman. Checking the living room and dining room brought smiles of satisfaction to her face. They were perfect, down to the coral-hued candles and napkins for dining, and the same touches for the aperitifs. Then she walked slowly into the living room. She still wasn't sure of her balance on the high heels, but they weren't uncomfortable.

When she heard Cas's key in the door, she took a deep breath and walked to the doorway to the foyer. She watched him as he stepped inside, seeing the tired look on his face, the quick glance he threw up the stairway.

"I'm here," she said. "Waiting for you."

His gaze slid over her, clinging. The tautness in his face eased some, and his smile was totally sensual. She smiled back.

"So you are," Cas murmured as he studied her. She was ravishing. She glinted with a thousand fires from her clothes to her hair, eyes and skin. "I have to trust my instincts here, Flame Lady."

"And what are they?" Hope bubbled in her. Some of the tension he'd displayed since the car accident had melted. It wasn't entirely dissipated, but it was a start.

"Either I'm being gloriously set up, or we've got a dinner engagement at Windsor Castle."

"Well, since you're so bright, I'll give you a hint. The queen has not invited us for dinner." When he pulled off his tie and dropped his briefcase, her knees turned liquid.

"I would've brought flowers," he whispered.

"You brought yourself. That's the best present in the world," she whispered back. Lord, he was unbuttoning his shirt, unzipping his fly. Her hands fluttered to her breast. Had there been a case of a heart beating so hard, it broke through the chest? "You needn't go up to change unless you wish. I've brought something down for you to wear."

"Give it to me. I want to shave . . . as quickly as I can, of course."

"Naturally." She hungered for him. She needed him. She returned to the living room for the silk kimono, then hurried back to him.

He almost fell over when he tried to push his trousers off over his shoes. "Damn! I'm so aroused, I'm clumsy."

Her answering chuckle was the most sensuous sound he'd ever heard.

"Hurry and change," she said. She couldn't seem to clear the huskiness from her voice. A little unsteady on the high heels, she walked back into the living room, crossing to the bar in the far corner. She retrieved the chilled champagne and set the bottle on the coffee table, in front of the fireplace. The hot canapés were in a chafing dish. She touched a match to the Sterno underneath, then bent over to arrange the other dishes for the tenth time. She didn't hear him enter the room until he whistled.

"Those heels and seraglio pants define your luscious body in wonderfully wicked ways, lady mine."

His whisper seemed to shiver up the backs of

her thighs, over her buttocks, up her spine to her neck. "Thank you." She threaded her hands together to stop their trembling.

"You are most welcome." He moved up behind her, his hands sliding and whispering over the satin as he embraced her and pressed his face to her hair. "Special occasion?"

She turned in his arms. "Yes and no."

"Enigmatic and oriental. That's my baby." He scrutinized her. He'd gotten in the habit of doing that since her accident on Fifth Avenue. He still couldn't totally eradicate his anger and fear. After all she'd been through, and then to be involved in an auto accident—

"Hey, come back to me." She could tell he was thinking about the accident again. She'd begun to realize that he'd somehow equated it with the plane crash. She pushed back from him and looked him up and down, imitating the way he'd looked at her, one finger stroking his freshly shaven skin. She looked at his hair. "You can't've showered too?"

"Quickie. I wanted to be fresh as the proverbial daisy for my lady." He fastened his hands to her waist, kneading gently. "Now, are you going to explain about tonight?"

She nodded. "I have something to tell you and something to ask you." She felt an infinitesimal stiffening. "All good things."

He buried his face in her neck. "Good. I like anything that won't part us."

She clung to him. "We'll never be parted again, love." She sensed he needed to hear that. And she needed to say it. She wasn't just removing any mask she had, she was flinging it far away, opening herself to the man she loved, leaving herself vulnerable. The same action might loosen what was left of Cas's own cover-up.

He shuddered against her. "Good."

She pushed back from him and led him to the sofa. The cool late-March evening called for a fire, and the burning apple logs gave off a heat and scent that made the room cozy, inviting, tailor-made for a twosome. When they were seated, she gestured toward the spears of broiled shark covered with hot fruit dip. "Taste." She gave him a plate and took one herself, then sat close to him.

He cupped his one arm around her. "Feed me from your plate, love." Lazy anticipation filled him. So far this seduction was wonderful.

"All right." When she'd lifted a spear to his mouth and he was chewing, she spoke. "Would you like to visit China—that is, Tibet?" Stupid, she berated herself. She'd dropped it like a bomb instead of leading up to it.

Cas stopped chewing. "Where did that question come from?" Wary, feeling threatened, he didn't take his eyes from her. Warm well-being began to seep away.

"Actually, Ione suggested it." Margo wanted to obliterate the whole subject in that second, bury it, forget it, get on with their lives any way they could. If opening up caused more wounds, could it be worth it? Taking a deep breath, she sat straighter and plunged on. "She said that you were still hurting, that you'd been hurt as much as I, only your cuts and bruises were on the inside and mine were primarily physical. I agree with her." She bit her lip, holding her breath. She'd really crossed the Rubicon this time.

"To a point, I agree too. But you were at death's door. I wasn't."

"But you bled from the thousand cuts that loss brings." She tried to smile. "I was so intent on your seeing how I'd changed and grown, and how I wanted our life to follow a pattern, that I almost forgot how devastated you were." She rubbed her finger over his freshly shaven face. He had wonderful skin.

Cas tried to pull her closer. "Yes, I was in a damned tailspin . . . and maybe I still am to some degree, but I can't compare it with what you went through."

She shook her head. "Not true." She put her index finger on his lips, smiling when he began to suck on it. "You were nearly destroyed, Cas. I know that now. I was so busy getting back to you, getting well for you, that I didn't even consider you'd need a long convalescence, too, that therapy could benefit you as it did me." She shook her head, battling the tears springing into her eyes. "I was coming home, fighting to get to you, but I didn't even see that you'd been on an odyssey too. I had a mask on, and blinders. And all the time I thought it was you in hiding, not me." A shaky sob escaped her. "It's taken me a while to get there, but I see your pain, Cas, and I want to eradicate it. I know we could both use the therapy of Tibet. We need to wipe the slate clean, my dear love, and we can do it together."

Cas nodded, his eyes moist. "Don't cry, sweetheart. Or you'll have me doing it."

Though she laughed, a tear spilled down her cheek. "I loved you then and I love you now." She kissed him gently, feeling his mouth quiver. "We really didn't know each other, Cas, but we will. It's so strange when I think of it. Not once did I consider that you could love me as much as I love you, that you could die if I did, when we were parted."

"I did die without you," he said gruffly, kissing another tear from her cheek.

"I know that now, my love. We were blind for a while, Cas."

"We had our masks on."

"Yes, yes, we did." She kissed his chin. "I want to tell you how I felt as I began to recover. From the very moment I knew I'd live, I began fighting my way back to you. It was my primary focus. Everything else was shunted aside. And when I found you, I was too enthralled with my own joy to see the horrible struggle you'd have to make to come back. Forgive me for not being as understanding as I should've been." She swiped at her tears. "It's taken me all this time to get some inkling into what you were and are going through."

"Ah, love, I never felt that you weren't understanding of me. But I will admit I did die. You were all of me, darling, and living without you was an eternal agony. I didn't belong anymore. I'd lost my entire blood system." His eyes had a faraway look. "When I discovered it was you, that you'd come back, I was so damned happy I almost collapsed . . . but I was afraid too. I knew what I'd become. My mind and body were swimming in booze. That was going to be my life. Work and forgetfulness." His smile was lopsided. "Then there you were, and I wasn't good enough for you. And I loved you so much."

"Yes, you were, Cas. You were always good enough."

Still smiling, he kissed her, taking her tongue into his mouth. When he lifted his head, they were still so close, they shared the same breaths. "No, I wasn't. I wanted you, but I wanted to be the man you expected me to be. I'd traveled a long way from the man you knew. And I didn't know if I could get back."

She nodded. "We both had to exorcise ghosts, and there are more to deal with, and we can do that. I want to take you to the Himalayas, show you where I crashed—"

"I've been there. I looked for you," he said abruptly. "I've no desire to see it again. I don't think I could go back." Time after time the images of the crash and the small hospital where he'd identified what he'd thought were her remains had risen in his mind like black specters. Hadn't he tried to banish it all from his mind? Dear Lord, how it hurt to dwell on it even for a moment. "I couldn't go back."

"Yes, yes, we both can. But this time it'll be different. We'll be together, finding our way back to each other on a newer, stronger path, knocking down and smashing the last of the barriers." She smiled, biting her lip. "And I'll be able to describe more clearly how I felt, show you so many things. You'll meet my mentor and you'll see where I stayed for so many months when I struggled to live, what was done to me and for me." She hurried her words, holding his hand between hers, her body swaying in intensity.

Cas heard the determination in her voice. "You've thought this all out, haven't you?" He could barely hide his trepidation, but under the layers of uncertainty he sensed she was right.

She nodded. "I think we need to go back and begin again, removing all the obstacles that impede the progress of our life."

Cas inhaled, then nodded slowly. "There are ghosts. But I don't relish going there. I've tried so hard to bury those awful months." He touched her cheek tenderly. "I suppose you'll want to go soon."

"'Ah, no. In about ten or eleven months should be about right."

"Ten or eleven months? Why so long?" The wariness that had become so much a part of him since the plane crash settled over him like a cloak. He braced himself. "Something's wrong. Right?"

She shook her head. "Actually, things are going smoothly. But you and I are having a baby in about seven months, and I think we should stay home and be with him or her before we take the trip."

Cas couldn't speak. He'd been holding his glass, but his hand started to shake so badly, he put it back on the table before he dropped it. Tentatively he touched Margo's middle. His hand trembled even more. "Are you sure?"

"I am. Isn't it great?" Laughter burst from her. "Weren't we practicing birth control?"

"I only knew I had to love you. I didn't take any precautions, not from the first time." He grimaced. "That was damned careless of me. Maybe it was on purpose. I sure as hell planned on keeping T'ang Qi, even before I loved her." He thrust his fingers through his hair, his glance skating over her. "I haven't asked, do you want this pregnancy?" Damn. He wanted the baby. A miniature of Margo.

"I do want it. Our baby will be perfect, or semi-perfect, or not so perfect, or pluperfect—"

"Are you strong enough?"

She saw the panic rise in his face. "My health is great. Don't forget I've been working out for more than a year now, steadily building my strength."

"I remember. T'ai chi." He put his head down to her middle, rubbing his cheek lightly against her. "I can't believe it. It's exciting." He lifted his head. "You won't want to leave the baby behind when we go to Tibet." He could almost feel the happiness and excitement bubbling through her. Her eagerness was infecting him.

"No, I won't. But I will. Perhaps I can prevail on T'ang to come to the States at some time to see his new progeny. That might be the only thing that would draw him here."

Cas nodded and straightened. "I'd like that. Then, when our child is old enough, he or she can return to Tibet to learn more of the ways of the lamas. Why are you crying?"

"Because you're no longer jealous of my mentor. Because of our love, and our openness with each other, you're beginning to see him with my eyes. You make me happy, Cas." No barriers could withstand their love. She could almost hear and feel the disintegration.

"Only fair. You gave my life meaning from the first moment. I came out of the water of the Seven Seas Lagoon and you were there, tugging on my hair. I looked into your eyes and fell in love. Those feelings haven't changed. If anything they've magnified." He squeezed her tight, turning his face into her body. "Oh, darling, you have to be well."

She tapped his cheek until he looked up at her. She saw the sheen of tears in his eyes. "I'm well, and I'll be even stronger before the birth. I intend to do all my exercises, all the time. Dannler even approved of the changes I want in our diet." Her heart almost stopped beating until he smiled. She wanted the child and she wanted Cas to want it, too.

"We'll exercise together and eat all the right foods."

"And you won't worry?" She didn't want those shadows in his eyes.

He shook his head, then nodded. "Yes, I'll worry. I can't help it. But we'll deal with that too."

She leaned toward him, kissing him. "We've knocked down a great many fences already, husband. And that's good. But sometimes it's good to stop talking. Like now." She nibbled at his chin, laughter bubbling up in her. "I'm going to have my wicked way with you, even without my brush and chisel."

He laughed. "Maybe we should get some curtains for that big window in your studio. We were pretty uninhibited."

"Nonsense. We need the north light . . . for everything." She pulled back a fraction. "Pregnancy makes me sexy. And I always feel sexy around you. You might be in trouble."

"I can handle it," he said hoarsely, then hauled her into his arms, kissing her deeply.

She gasped when he pulled back then leaned down and took her breast into his mouth, right through the silk top! Shivers raced up and down her spine until she was a mass of goose-bumps from head to toe. When Cas began whispering all the erotic things he was going to do to her, all night long, Margo turned to liquid, sagging against him, loving him, wanting him.

He lifted his head, smiling at her. Then, easing back from her, he edged the coffee table away from the couch and fire, tipping a plate of dip. When Margo giggled, he shrugged. "So I'm a little messy."

"Dannler'll get ya," she chided, eyeing the space he'd made for them on the oriental rug and sliding toward him. She reached out and found him hard. When his eyes glittered over her, she couldn't stem the moan that broke from her. "Cas."

"Yes, Margo, I'm here." He moved off the couch and scooped her down beside him. Sliding to a supine position, he pulled her on top of him, on her back. He inhaled her essence, his eyes closing.

"You're breathing in my ear," she whispered. "It turns me on."

"That's the idea, wife."

He was on fire for her himself. His hands stroked over her silky top, the hissing sound made an erotic stimulus to his already overheated blood. When she wriggled against him, a sexual ache welled up in him, swelling into a thundering fury of want. His hands feathered over her, then slipped inside her loose trousers. He touched her at the sweet junction of her body. She was hot and wet for him, and they'd just started. He twined his fingers in the soft mat of curls, then slipped them between the soft, wet lips of her lower body. He began a rhythm that her hips answered. She gasped and made soft mewing sounds in her throat. Desperate to touch him, she tried to turn.

"Don't move like that, darling," he warned her. "Or it will be over before it's begun."

Smiling at her husky laugh, he lifted her body and edged the silky lounge pants down her legs, caressing her skin as the light material whispered over her feet. "Umm, those undies. The same color as your pajamas. Very sexy."

"Thank you." Out of breath, giddy with wanting him, she waited as though she were poised on the edge of a precipice. She felt like yelling at him to hurry, yet she loved his languorous motions. The hot, abrasively sexy hesitations of those wonderful hands drove her wild.

He cupped her breasts, his thumb pressing and caressing her nipples. One hand slipped downward and returned to the hot wetness between her thighs. Pleasure rippled through him. When he felt her shudder, his delight increased a thousandfold.

"I hope you're not too tired tonight, angel," he murmured. "Because it should take me all night to kiss every pore and I intend to do just that." Lifting her again, he turned her and settled her down on top of him, their faces touching.

"I'll nap tomorrow," she said dazedly.

Their open mouths met in a hungry kiss, tongues dueling, lips pressed hard to one another. Margo wrapped her arms around his neck, her naked body rubbing up and down against him, her questioning moans demanding he remove his clothes.

Cas freed himself, then stripped, tossing his garments every which way. Then, body to body, they undulated against each other. "I'm going to love you, wife of mine."

"And I'm going to love you. I always have." His smile was sparked with sensuality, making the blood thunder through her. Margo groaned, kissing him again, holding him tightly to her. When he slipped downward, pressing his face in the valley of her breasts, she sucked in a sharp breath. It was all sweetly familiar, and all brand-new. His mouth was sliding from one breast to the other, laving, loving, licking the nipple taut and red. She tried to remain still to savor the lovemaking, but her body denied her and began a rhythm of its own. Crying out in pleasure, she clung to his shoulders when he kissed her navel, his tongue whorling around it, his hands kneading her middle, hotly caressing her stomach . . . and lower.

Air was tortured in her lungs, but she couldn't get a breath when he pulled the sweet junction of her body up tight against his mouth, stroking her with his tongue, taking her, giving her such pleasure that her body and mind spasmed in delight, and she didn't know if she were on the rug or floating to the ceiling. She should have been used to Cas's power, but it was frighteningly monumental. "Cas! I can't—"

"Shh, love, there's more."

"No! My turn." She slid down his body, caressing and kissing him. She took hold of his aroused body, placing her mouth over it, giving him the love that he gave her. She lifted slumberous eyes and smiled at him. "Do you like it?"

"Yes," he said, his voice cracking. Kettledrums were pounding in his head. He was nearing the breaking point. "Darling!" He whipped her up his body, sliding smoothly inside her. The connection made, he sighed, just as she did. Stillness. They looked into each other's eyes.

"I love you, wife."

He thrust upward with one forceful surge. When she cried out, he opened his eyes, but he saw that her head was back and that she was in the throes of sexual fulfillment. He let go, spiraling into the vortex with her. Climbing, climbing, they drove through the stars to the unknown universe where only lovers go, exploding their own black hole of delight, meteors cascading all around them.

They lay there, holding each other, buried in each other, loath to let go of the power.

"Loving you is so aerobic," Margo said, yawning.

Cas stiffened. "Are you all right? I didn't think you were hurt."

She opened one eye, her smile lopsided. "Cas, you could only hurt me if you left me. You just loved me. I'm happy."

He grinned. "You were very good, Mrs. Griffith. Who taught you all those love variations you do so well?"

Her eyes snapped open, but she didn't see any anger in his expression, only lazy satisfaction. "You taught me. Have you forgotten?"

"I think I need to be reminded all the time."

She laughed. "Sounds good. I could use as much of it as you can share."

He rolled over, his body tenting hers. "Oh, lady, you don't know what you're in for now."

"Oh, yeah?" Giggles erupted out of her. She put her hand over her mouth, but she couldn't stem the mirth.

"What's this? Somebody tickling you?" His hands danced over her middle, and he couldn't help laughing.

"Stop it!" she cried, trying to get free, trying to retaliate.

Gales of laughter rolled out of him, and he collapsed on top of her, bracing himself with his arms.

Hanging on to him, she continued laughing, tears raining down her face. Finally they were holding each other and shaking with amusement.

"Sex is certainly fun," Margo managed to say, before going off into more hilarity.

"Damn your silliness. I love you, woman." Cas was still laughing when he kissed her over and over again.

Nine

The top of the world was mountains and deep snow. The sun's glitter stung the eyes. Breathing was ice crystals formed in every exhalation. Silence was the whistling wind that whirled the snow into air spouts. The world was lonely, white, craggy, awesome.

"What do you think?" Margo asked, standing next to her husband as he gazed out the window of the lamasery's main room. She held her breath, patting her tummy as she'd been doing every so often since the birth of the twins. She couldn't get used to the flatness!

"The view is almost as beautiful as you, but not quite," Cas said simply. "You're the most beautiful woman in the world, and the mother of Celia Ione and Lancaster Ivor Griffith. Have I told you how proud I am of you?"

"Only a million times, but I still like to hear it." Margo felt wonderful. If she felt trepidation at the thought of the impending meeting between the two men dearest to her in the world, she tamped down the sensation. The last months with Cas had been wonderful. He was a doting father who couldn't get enough of his son and daughter. They'd been left with Ivor and Ione and a phalanx of first-class nurses.

Cas smiled. "I still get a little shaky when I think of our children's births, but I'm getting better."

"I'm sure you won't be allowed in that hospital again. Giving orders like a sea captain, and instructing everyone within hearing on their duties."

Cas grimaced. "I was a little upset."

Neither heard the slap of the silk slippers until the man they'd come to see was next to them.

"T'ang!" Margo launched herself into his arms, almost unbalancing her mentor. She brushed away her tears as she studied him. "You look the same."

"And you look different, my child. Well loved and loving, content. You've achieved your great quest. Have you not?" T'ang didn't wait for an answer. He turned to smile at Cas, and bow. "And you are her Cas, whom she called out to so many times when she was ill and edging so close to death."

Cas flushed with pleasure and nodded. "I've come to learn, as she did."

T'ang nodded. "It's good. Some of what you learn will pain you, but it will be a good cleansing pain." He stopped and looked at Margo for a long moment. "And when you return home, I shall join you to see my new children. But now you will have tea and rest." T'ang smiled at Cas. "Already you've learned many things. When my child was in danger, you felt the messages I sent you and went after her. You are a family with my child and me. It's good." T'ang left as quietly as he'd come.

Cas was astounded. "He sent me that message, the day of the accident?"

Margo nodded. "He knows many things. He's kind and wise and honorable, and I will always love and revere him."

Cas looked at her, his eyes moist. "He's wonderful, and I thank him for telling me about the danger you were in, love."

"I told you we were connected." She took her husband's arm and led him from the room and up the winding stair to their starkly simple bedchamber. "He likes you," she said excitedly when Cas closed the door behind them. "And he's coming to us in New York. He knew I was going to ask him. I hardly dared hope . . ." She bit her lip, trying not to cry. "Oh, Cas, my darling, our world comes together here where we truly found each other, though we were thousands of miles apart."

He nodded. "I know that now, love."

"The masks are truly off and we can see each other. I'm silly to cry, husband, when I'm so happy." The tears on her cheeks mirrored the ones on his as he opened his arms to her.

"I love you, Margo, far more than I ever thought I could. And there will never be a mask between us again, love. I look forward to our life and all we can teach each other."

"I love you, husband."

They kissed, fusing their mouths, their love, and their lives.

And the masks melted away, never to be seen again.

THE EDITOR'S CORNER

Each month we have LOVESWEPTs that dazzle . . . that warm the heart or bring laughter and the occasional tear—all of them sensual and full of love, of course. Seldom, however, are all six books literally sizzling with so much fiery passion and tumultuous romance as next month's.

First, a love story sure to blaze in your memory is remarkable Billie Green's **STARBRIGHT,** LOVESWEPT #456. Imagine a powerful man with midnight-blue eyes and a former model who has as much heart and soul as she does beauty. He is brilliant lawyer Garrick Fane, a man with a secret. She is Elise Adler Bright, vulnerable and feisty, who believes Garrick has betrayed her. When a terrifying accident hurls them together, they have one last chance to explore their fierce physical love . . . and the desperate problems each has tried to hide. As time runs out for them, they must recapture the true love they'd once believed was theirs—or lose it forever. Fireworks sparked with humor. A sizzler, indeed.

Prepare to soar when you read LOVESWEPT #457, **PASSION'S FLIGHT,** by talented Terry Lawrence. Sensual, sensual, sensual is this story of a legendary dancer and notorious seducer known throughout the world as "Stash." He finds the woman he can love faithfully for a lifetime in Mariah Heath. Mariah is also a dancer and one Stash admires tremendously for her grace and fierce emotionality. But he is haunted by a past that closes him to enduring love—and Mariah must struggle to break through her own vulnerabilities to teach her incredible lover that forever can be theirs. This is a romance that's as unforgettable as it is delectable.

As steamy as the bayou, as exciting as Bourbon Street in New Orleans, **THE RESTLESS HEART,** LOVESWEPT #458, by gifted Tami Hoag, is sure to win your heart. Tami has really given us a gift in the hero she's created for this romance. What a wickedly handsome, mischievous, and sexy Cajun Remy Doucet is! And how he woos heroine Danielle Hamilton. From diapering babies to kissing a lady senseless, Remy is masterful. But a lie and a shadow stand between him and Danielle . . . and only when a dangerous misunderstanding parts them can they find truth and the love they deserve. Reading not to be missed!

Guaranteed to start a real conflagration in your imagination is extraordinary Sandra Chastain's **FIREBRAND,** LOVESWEPT #459. Cade McCall wasn't the kind of man to answer an ad as mysterious as Rusty Wilder's—but he'd never needed a job so badly. When he met the green-eyed rancher whose wild red hair echoed her spirit, he fell hard. Rusty found Cade too handsome, too irresistible to become the partner she needed. Consumed by the flames of desire they generated, only searing romance could follow . . . but each feared their love might turn to ashes if he or she couldn't tame the other. Silk and denim . . . fire and ice. A LOVESWEPT that couldn't have been better titled—**FIREBRAND**.

Delightful Janet Evanovich outdoes herself with **THE ROCKY ROAD TO ROMANCE,** LOVESWEPT #460, which sparkles with fiery fun. In the midst of a wild and woolly romantic chase between Steve Crow and Daisy Adams, you should be prepared to meet an old and fascinating friend—that quirky Elsie Hawkins. This is Elsie's fourth appearance in Janet's LOVESWEPTS. All of us have come to look forward to where she'll turn up next . . . and just how she'll affect the outcome of a stalled romance. Elsie won't disappoint you as she works her wondrous ways on the smoldering romance of Steve and Daisy. A real winner!

Absolutely breathtaking! A daring love story not to be missed! Those were just a couple of the remarks heard in the office from those who read **TABOO**, LOVESWEPT #461, by Olivia Rupprecht. Cammie Walker had been adopted by Grant Kennedy's family when her family died in a car crash. She grew up with great brotherly love for Grant. Then, one night when Cammie came home to visit, she saw Grant as she'd never seen him before. Her desire for him was overwhelming . . . unbearably so. And Grant soon confessed he'd been passionately in love with her for years. But Cammie was terrified of their love . . . and terrified of how it might affect her adopted parents. **TABOO** is one of the most emotionally touching and stunningly sensual romances of the year.

And do make sure you look for the three books next month in Bantam's fabulous imprint, FANFARE . . . the very best in women's popular fiction. It's a spectacular FANFARE month with **SCANDAL** by Amanda Quick, **STAR-CROSSED LOVERS** by Kay Hooper, and **HEAVEN SENT** by newcomer Pamela Morsi.

Enjoy!

Sincerely,

Carolyn Nichols

Carolyn Nichols,
Publisher,
LOVESWEPT
Bantam Books
666 Fifth Avenue
New York, NY 10103

THE LATEST IN BOOKS
AND AUDIO CASSETTES

Paperbacks

☐	28671	**NOBODY'S FAULT** Nancy Holmes	$5.95
☐	28412	**A SEASON OF SWANS** Celeste De Blasis	$5.95
☐	28354	**SEDUCTION** Amanda Quick	$4.50
☐	28594	**SURRENDER** Amanda Quick	$4.50
☐	28435	**WORLD OF DIFFERENCE** Leonia Blair	$5.95
☐	28416	**RIGHTFULLY MINE** Doris Mortman	$5.95
☐	27032	**FIRST BORN** Doris Mortman	$4.95
☐	27283	**BRAZEN VIRTUE** Nora Roberts	$4.50
☐	27891	**PEOPLE LIKE US** Dominick Dunne	$4.95
☐	27260	**WILD SWAN** Celeste De Blasis	$5.95
☐	25692	**SWAN'S CHANCE** Celeste De Blasis	$5.95
☐	27790	**A WOMAN OF SUBSTANCE** Barbara Taylor Bradford	$5.95

Audio

☐ **SEPTEMBER** by Rosamunde Pilcher
Performance by Lynn Redgrave
180 Mins. Double Cassette 45241-X $15.95

☐ **THE SHELL SEEKERS** by Rosamunde Pilcher
Performance by Lynn Redgrave
180 Mins. Double Cassette 48183-9 $14.95

☐ **COLD SASSY TREE** by Olive Ann Burns
Performance by Richard Thomas
180 Mins. Double Cassette 45166-9 $14.95

☐ **NOBODY'S FAULT** by Nancy Holmes
Performance by Geraldine James
180 Mins. Double Cassette 45250-9 $14.95

- - - - - - - - - - - - - - - - - -

Bantam Books, Dept. FBS, 414 East Golf Road, Des Plaines, IL 60016

Please send me the items I have checked above. I am enclosing $_____
(please add $2.50 to cover postage and handling). Send check or money order,
no cash or C.O.D.s please. (Tape offer good in USA only.)

Mr/Ms _____

Address _____

City/State _____ Zip _____

FBS–1/91

Please allow four to six weeks for delivery.
Prices and availability subject to change without notice.

60 Minutes to a Better, More Beautiful You!

Now it's easier than ever to awaken your sensuality, stay slim forever—even make yourself irresistible. With Bantam's bestselling subliminal audio tapes, you're only 60 minutes away from a better, more beautiful you!

__ 45004-2	**Slim Forever**	$8.95
__ 45035-2	**Stop Smoking Forever**	$8.95
__ 45022-0	**Positively Change Your Life**	$8.95
__ 45041-7	**Stress Free Forever**	$8.95
__ 45106-5	**Get a Good Night's Sleep**	$7.95
__ 45094-8	**Improve Your Concentration**	$7.95
__ 45172-3	**Develop A Perfect Memory**	$8.95

Bantam Books, Dept. LT, 414 East Golf Road, Des Plaines, IL 60016

Please send me the items I have checked above. I am enclosing $_____ (please add $2.50 to cover postage and handling). Send check or money order, no cash or C.O.D.s please. (Tape offer good in USA only.)

Mr/Ms _____

Address _____

City/State _____ Zip _____

LT-2/91

Please allow four to six weeks for delivery.
Prices and availability subject to change without notice.

NEW!

Handsome Book Covers Specially Designed To Fit Loveswept Books

Our new French Calf Vinyl book covers come in a set of three great colors— royal blue, scarlet red and kachina green.

Each 7" × 9½" book cover has two deep vertical pockets, a handy sewn-in bookmark, and is soil and scratch resistant.

To order your set, use the form below.

ORDER FORM

STX

YES! Please send me

_____ set(s) of three book covers at $5.95 per set. Enclosed is my check/money order for the full amount. (Price includes postage and handling; NY and IL residents, please add appropriate sales tax.) 09605

Ship To:

_____

Name   (Please Print)

_____

Address

_____

City   State   Zip

Send Order To: Bantam Books, Merchandise Division
                P.O. Box 956
                Hicksville, NY 11802

Prices in U.S. dollars   Satisfaction Guaranteed
                                          STX—3/87